Journey's End

Ron Mueller

<u>Books by Ron Mueller</u>

The Savitar Series-Science Fiction
Journey's End
Savitar
Confluence

Bram Nielson Series-Science Fiction
The Fold
The Message
Fold Wormhole
Negative Fold
Ripples in Time

The Alex Evercrest Series-Detective
The River Front
The Girl on the Grill
Missing
Maggot
Racist
Votive Candles
Windy City
Country Road
Pool of Blood
Sins of the Daughter

The Taelo Series-Prehistory America
Taelo: The Early Years
Taelo: The Golden Feather
Taelo: Journey of Discovery
Taelo: Dangerous Passage
Taelo: Condor Clan Slingers
Taelo: Circumvention
Taelo: The Journey of Sages

A Taelo Story
The Name of the Child
White Swan and Quiet Pheasant
Broken Spear
Floating Cloud
Quiet Rabbit
Busy Bee
Little Otter& Talking Wren
Burley Bear & Meadow Flower

A Feather-in-the-Wind Story
The Eastern Elk Clan

The Door Series-Science Fiction
The Door
Delivery
Journey Beyond

The Problem Solver Series-Secret Agent
The Beginning
Drug Lords
Broder Crosser

Current Past and Future-Science Fiction
Event Survivors-Science Fiction
The Door-Science Fiction
Viajante 7-Science Fiction
Imagination - Courtney Huynh & Chloe Parker

Journey's End

By: *Ron Mueller*

Around the World Publishing LLC
4914 Cooper Road Suite 144
Cincinnati, Ohio 45242-9998

This story is a work of fiction. Names, characters, places, and incidents either are products of the author's imagination or are used fictitiously. Any resemblance to actual events or locales or persons, living or dead, is entirely coincidental.

Journey's End, by Ron Mueller Copyright © 2019
Renewed 2023

ISBN 13: 978-1-68223-303-0
ISBN 10: 1-68223-303-0

Cover Design By: Ron Mueller

Table of Content

Ron Mueller

Journey's End

Chapter 1: In the Dark of the night

The crawl from the sea, the lunge forward with the first breath of air, the death burning rays of day, the healing power of the night, and the life-giving cover of the caves all floated out of the soprano's voice in a haunting descant over the thundering drums engulfed the rapturous audience. It cascaded across the audience half out of their seats and swaying with every word like a wave on the beach overwhelms those standing in its way.

The words, the voice, the drums carried everyone through the path, the maze, and the pain of their history.

The giant meteor's impact on the planet was echoed by the deep thundering drums and the deep voice of the bassoon. The cracking of the planet's mantle and dramatic altering of the magnetic field were accented in piercing howls of pain and the crashing of the large thunderous hanging gongs.

A thunderous voice rose and went on to tell how nature ignored the formidable damage and miraculously created and expanded life in the incredibly deep water filled canyons that the impact had created. These deep canyons were made by the impact of the asteroid and the splitting of the planets mantle. Most of the Home Orb's water flowed into these canyons but much of the water was lost to space.

From the beginning, the night and shadow became the nurturer and the Sun's unfiltered rays the extinguisher of life. This was due to the fact that, the ravaged atmosphere was too shallow, and the distorted magnetic field too weak, to shield the planet from the stream of sterilizing radiation flowing out from the Sun. Life evolved by embracing the night and by keeping to the depths of the radiation shielding canyons.

Life struggled mightily, but slowly, in millions of years, achieved sentience and intelligence. The struggle for survival was excruciatingly intense and the survivors were few.

As far back as recorded history could be traced, the population held a celebration of their origin, after each rotation around the Grand Orb. The audience in attendance all breathed in the words, leaned slowly forward and then back swaying in unison with the singer in the spotlight.

The singers shadowed eyes juxtaposed against the brightness of the light signified the battle between the Sun and the shadow in the depth of their canyons. This was the story of survival, the story of life and the story of death. This was an ancient story of love, of family and of hope.

There was no other way. All of them were proof of the fortitude and the passion for life their ancestors and they all embraced. They were the proof that the agony of their ancestors had not yielded to the damage to their Orb but had flourished in spite of every barrier that had seemed determined to stop them.

Nadia and her close friends were enjoying this celebration. This was a central part of this close-knit group's annual outing. All had been classmates and friends at university of Ulm. They were now in a variety of professional and technical fields.

Nadia had followed her father into the field of Astronomy and was currently Second Chairman of Astronomy at Ulm University. She was the youngest to have achieved this position. She was never idle and was always seeking new discovery. She was at her telescope every moment of the night. She had inherited her father's passion for the universe. She was as relentless and demanding as he and had the advantage of the work that had been achieved in both the analysis and the telescope equipment during the time she was growing up.

Her mind was struggling to stay in the moment. The troubling discovery from the previous work cycle were tugging at her and she could not get fully into the flow of the early morning revelry. She was worried and really wanted to be back in her office so she could continue the analysis that she had already been through several times and had given her results that she could not believe.

She followed her friends as they left the theater thoroughly enjoying the morning. She knew the next part of their celebration was their tram ride across to the other side of the canyon. On the far side they would go up the side of the canyon to point that the shadow and the light from Grand Orb first met as the Orb ascended above the canyon.

Then in a show of camaraderie and defiance they would put their hands together into the light of rising Orb. This was their show of victory against the burning radiation of the Grand Orb.

As Nadia extended her hand a shiver of despair ran up her back and caused the light down hairs on her skin to stand on end. There was a foreboding feeling in her mind. She could not let it go. The foreboding was overwhelming.

She was lost in thought about an unusual observation she had made during the previous night's work cycle. She wondered about what she had discovered at the outer region of Orb's orbital system.

Some immense force was causing a disruption in the trajectory of three asteroids. This force was beyond anything known to her or ever reported by the Astronomers at Ulm.

It was hard for her to concentrate on the events of the morning and her friends.

She was with them physically, but her mind was racing on ahead trying to make sense out of what she was sure was a troubling new discovery. She was continually re-analyzing the data. There had to be a mistake. She would need to re-examine everything. She must have made a mistake.

"Hey, star gazer, are you still with us?" one of the group called to her as he held the door of the tram so she could get on board.

She knew that the party would go long into the day cycle. Later they would all wonder why they had stayed out for so long. For now, they were together and having fun. They only did this once a seasonal cycle and they intended to maximize their fun.

This rest cycle, Nadia excused herself early and went to get as much sleep as she could. She had to give her mind time to recover from the night of analysis.

Nadia's rest cycle had indeed been cut short by the partying.

Early in the evening, a little on the exhausted side, Nadia left her apartment and took the elevator to the surface. The Grand Orb's rays were making their final attempt at lighting the sky. It was sinking below the far horizon as she walked to the edge of the canyon to her favorite spot.

Nadia made it a point to always walk to work in the evening shadows. The walk connected her with the surface of her Orb and the view of the multitude of stars in the sky. She looked up at the stars and absorbed the black expanse of space. A cool evening breeze ruffled her hair and caressed her reddish down covered skin. The setting of the Grand Orb was her favorite time of the waking cycle.

For her it marked a beginning.

She had walked this path many times. She and her father were regular visitors. In the not-so-distant past, she had asked to be walked to school via the surface. Nadia adored her father and had listened, had learned and then she followed his footsteps in her career as an astronomer.

This evening she knew she needed him more than ever. Her foreboding discovery of the black void weighed heavily on her. The void was unexplainable. It was a new phenomenon. There was no reference book to read to gain understanding. She felt that the very existence of her world could be at stake.

She would call for her father's help but only if her work team verified her finding. He was a force she only wanted to engage when everything that could be checked had been checked.

She stopped to watch as the observatory rose slowly up from below the surface. It reminded her of the mushrooms her mother was developing. One could watch this new species of mushrooms grow.

Given sufficient nutrients and light the mushroom would sprout and reach full size during one work cycle. The observatory was lowered during daylight to protect the equipment and the people inside from the radiation streaming out from the Grand Orb.

The radiation shield for the observatory was a disk that was lowered into place and filled with water. It was at twenty feet deep and was sufficient to shield the people who worked the day shift. The day shift was used for maintenance, repair, and clean-up.

Once the Grand Orb set the night cycle was used to make celestial observations, to gather data and to do analysis. The darkness of the night quickly followed the setting Grand Orb. As she walked toward the elevator, the stars were coming to their full brilliance. Nadia loved the sheer overwhelming number of stars showing across the entire nightscape.

She was almost always alone on this walk. She wished otherwise but no one had become close enough to her to be asked to make the walk with her. Most personnel entered the observatory via the underground entrance elevators.

The observatory was part of the University of Ulm. Ulm was one of the largest and oldest communities on the planet. The city began at least two hundred feet underground and continued down for at least another ten thousand feet. The University was built as the top-most, layer of the city. It lay in ten huge chambers with the observatory almost directly in the center.

The city of Ulm was a vertical community with the production and manufacturing done at the lower levels. Food processing facilities were carved into the mantel at the lowest levels of the canyon. Above them were the manufacturing facilities. Above the manufacturing facilities were the living quarters. Finally, above the living quarters was Ulm University. The low-grade heat from lower levels was used to maintain a comfortable temperature in the living areas. This layout proved to be the most efficient use of energy and it optimized the management of utilities and waste.

Nadia marveled at the practical design that had been put in place by her ancestors and that had been continually improved as technology advanced.

Ulm was a closed environment. Everything was recycled and only periodically was water taken from the canyon seas. Fresh food was grown in the shadows of the canyon. Many of the required nutrients were mined from deep inside the mantle. The food crops were part of the recycling system.

The digging for nutrients was part of the slowly expanding housing for the slowly growing Ulm population.

Nadia embraced the design, construction, and maintenance of the Ulm system as a testament to the capabilities of their race.

The ancients originally used natural caves to shelter themselves from the radiation. Slowly they carved additional spaced into the stone itself.

The ability to create their own shelter and escape from the deadly radiation gave the ancients the dominant position on the planet. Over the thousands of years, they continued the expansion of Ulm.

Eventually some hardy explorers climbed up out of the deep canyon of Ulm and searched for other habitable areas. This expansion across the mantel to discover other deep fracture canyons took several thousands of years. Slowly the daring and adventuresome followed and established the newer communities of New Ulm, Yalton, Ranter, Walen and Hueval.

Each new community was roughly one thousand years after the other. Over six thousand years the base of the population was established. Together these six deep canyons now supported one billion inhabitants. Ulm was the oldest and the largest with a population of three hundred million. The population level of each of the subsequent canyons was less and was based on their size and years of existence. All were at the limits of the population they could support.

Ulm was by far the largest of all the canyons.

The six canyons were now connected by through the mantle tunnels. These were first cut through by shear will and muscle power. Over the many years as technology improved the tunnels continued to be expanded. These tunnels had grown to the point where at present the tunnels themselves housed at least a million families. A high speed, through the mantle transit system now served to connect the six canyons.

Ulm enjoyed the luxury of a park of green grasses, bushes, and flowers. The park was a long and narrow ribbon bordering the farmlands. The farmland extended up to the radiation boarder high on the other side of the canyon.

The city of Ulm was built into the mantel on the side considered to be the radiation shade side.

The park was the only external extravagant feature Ulm displayed. The rest of the canyon was efficiently developed to provide the maximum farmland. Immense terraces rose up the sides of the canyon. The exterior space was critical to grow the plants that provided the sustenance for the entire population.

Ulm was the major and most productive grower of food. Each of the other canyons produced food as well but their terraces were just being developed and they were slowly increasing capacity as they increased the radiation shielding of their canyons.

As Ulm grew in size, the excavation went deeper and deeper back into the mantle. The excavated material was used to build new and enhance the existing farming terraces. A large amount was taken up to the top of the canyon to increase the height of the radiation shielding wall. The fabricated wall shaded the canyon to the point the terraces climbed more than halfway up the opposite sided of the canyon wall. The radiation shielding height was almost at the optimum.

Much higher and not enough light would be available for the lower farmland. Plants needed the sunlight, but they could not withstand the radiation that came with it. It was a balancing act that had been learned over the thousands of years.

The other cities around the planet followed the example set by Ulm. The additional farmland allowed the population to achieve a new level of prosperity and comfort.

As far as Nadia knew, the Orbians were the only sentient beings in the solar system, and they were the only large land dwellers. What remained on land were a few protected creatures living out in the terrace walls.

There were also some protected water creatures still in existence. The precarious nature of their own existence overcame the guilt they as a population felt for failing to save more of the other species. Not only had their ancestors overcome their crawl out from the sea but they had to overcome the deadly radiation streaming in to sterilize the planet.

The meager plant life at the very depths of the canyons in the cracked mantel barely served to sustain the initial meager numbers of their race. The other species lost the competition early in the history of the Orb and became extinct long before the sentience of the population understood the situation.

Time was measured against a single cycle of their Orb around the Grand Orb. This was divided into fourteen equal periods.

Each rotation of their Orb was divided into twenty time periods.

The Grand Orb in the sky sent everyone inward and most to sleep. When it was dark, surface work took place. This night work was driven by the need to avoid the high day time radiation exposure.

Much of the success of their species was the evolution of the very fast radiation damage repair capability of their bodies. High radiation exposure was quickly overcome by hiding in the mantle and giving their body time to repair the damage. Even so they evolved to using the night to work and the day to sleep. They were not creatures of the night for they used bright lights in the fields and throughout the canyon to facilitate the work.

It was the unfiltered radiation from the Grand Orb that every creature on the planet hid from.

The geological history of the planet was something all students learned in their early years. The gigantic comet or asteroid collision with the planet changed the rotation and the position of the interior metal core and greatly weakened the planets magnetic field.

The force of the impact cracked the mantle and created the deep crevasses now housing all life.

Whether it accelerated or devastated evolution was still heatedly debated by the scholars. Most thought it had accelerated evolution by eliminating all but a few creatures. The theory held these creatures were stressed in their need to survive. This stress accelerated the development of intelligence.

Nadia had no clue as to the rightness or correctness of any of the positions. She understood history and once having understood it, she looked to the future and how her race might sustain what was left.

Nadia's parents both graduates from Ulm and were globally recognized for their advanced astronomical and biological work. They always encouraged Nadia and her older brother Keren to go to Ulm University.

Nadia's choice of Astronomy was influenced by her close relationship with her father.

Her first walk with him along the top of the Canyon to look at the stars awakened one of her passions. Nadia had learned much from her father, but she was now recognized for her own talent. She graduated number one in her undergraduate class and went on to get her PhD.

A position at the observatory followed. Nadia's current project in the observatory was the study of asteroids and comets making their way across the vast space of the solar system.

Her second and inner passion was to sing! She had been singing all her life. She wrote her own lyrics. These were on a wide variety of topics, but one repeating theme was for the Orbians to reach for the stars. She was seldom without a song on her lips. Several of her songs were popular across the Orb. She still wrote and sang songs and her public eagerly bought and listened to what she produced.

Her singing provided her a lucrative income. Her work at the observatory provided her time to think of new lyrics.

Her passion for music made her more money than her passion for the stars.

Her two passions complemented each other. Nadia was one of the few to enjoy solitude as much as she enjoyed being with friends and family. The number and closeness of all the population was directly reflected in the culture of families living in the same unit all their lives. Seldom was anyone alone.

Unlike most of her friends Nadia lived alone. Her normal routine was to finish work, go to her apartment, listen to, or write music, do some exercise, read, and finally fall asleep. Every ten or twelve work cycles she would spend time with her family. This family time was precious to her, and she looked forward to it. The family would spend two or three work cycles together. It was Nadia's family custom for each family member to take a turn planning some major family outing.

Nadia recalled a list of the most recent family events, a moonlight outing on the beach, a day light outing on the valley floor to wander through the green forest, a submarine excursion to the bottom of the sea, the tunnel train trips to the other canyons on the planet. There was a map on the family room wall of all the places and the things they had done together.

They even entered a family singing contest and placed third. It was at this event where she won an award for her single vocal and became an instant hit throughout the Orb. It was a standing joke she obtained her degree in astronomy because she thought it was the only way she was going to be with the stars instead she had become one!

Nadia brought herself out of her reverie and continued her walk to the observatory. As she waited for the elevator doors to open, she glanced once more to the stars. The polished metal of the elevator allowed her to study herself. She was tall and slender. She stood a good half ahead above her father. Her large black pupils and yellow eyes were her mothers. Nadia claimed her sharp white teeth and smile were hers. She was a contrast to her brother who was a good head shorter.

He was broader, heavier, and stronger than she. He had almost grey eyes from her father's family. He was more serious but still a lot of fun to be around. He had always been her "protector" though there was nothing to protect her from.

Nadia entered the observatory. Her team had the dome open and the telescope up and in position. They knew Nadia would not talk to them until she had gone through her ritual of viewing the asteroids.

She raised the viewing scope as she adjusted the controls to point at the location in the sky where she had last seen the largest asteroid. She looked into the eye piece. The act of looking was not a necessary step. The computer was capable of locating and verifying the location of the asteroid and displaying it on a large screen.

Nadia, however, always started and ended the day by personally locating and seeing the object. This was a quirk she had inadvertently adopted years ago from her father.

She had spent countless hours reviewing the trajectory analysis of the three objects she was following. They could not have changed course unless these three objects were powered, or unless something was attracting them. If the objects were powered there should be some sort of energy signature. There was no energy signature. Her check confirmed all three objects had changed course at roughly the same point and once again they were together on their new trajectory. What could have caused this change in direction? She had either found space travelers or there was some other unknown force causing these objects change direction.

During her previous work cycle, she had suspected a common flaw in the sensors or in the data she was using.

She had ended the previous work cycle in a confused state. She concluded that her data was corrupted.

The revelation as to the cause of the change in the course of the three asteroids came to her during the celebration with her friends. When she extended her hand into the Grand Orb, she knew she had discovered an unknown force. You could not see the sunlight strike your skin, but you could feel the heat. In the case of asteroids, she could not see the force, but you could see its effects. Something closed to the magnitude of the Grand Orb must be the cause!

She ended her visual observation and called her team together.

Each of her team members had gone to their analysis terminals in the observatory. Technology had changed the observatory to look more like a computer room than an observatory.

They gathered at the central meeting table.

"I have a serious assignment I want you to tackle as a team. Please plot the trajectory of the three asteroids I have been tracking. Verify the change of trajectory. Determine how they could change trajectory. Estimate the force required to make this trajectory change. This will be everyone's work until you as a team report back.

Meetil, you are in charge of the team. Are there any questions? Nadia waited few moments then continued, "Ok, call me when you are through. It's okay to work together. This is not a test."

Nadia left her team as they discussed how to organize to do the analysis she had requested. She was off to look out ahead of the asteroids in search of the source of the force attracting them. Her estimates of this force put it beyond anything she had ever been taught or studied. What she had calculated the evening before was impossible. It would rival the power of the Grand Orb!

Nadia thought of her father. She needed his insight and guidance. She would call him when her team confirmed her discovery. She missed his collaboration but his focus on the third Orb from the Grand Orb now absorbed all his time.

Nadia was a little jealous of her father's fixation. He had moved his office out to the new space center, and she missed their walks along the top of the canyon.

She suspected he had moved in order to be far enough away to give her the space she needed to make her own way.

Chapter 2: Raulens

*R*aulens was the only child in his family. This was the norm because there was a one child policy in place that strictly enforced.

His father was a farmer, which meant that he worked during the night.

His mother was a librarian at Ulm University. Since the library was shielded and deep in the mantle she worked during the day as well.

This choice synchronized the three of their wake cycle.

She often brought Raulens to work with her. He loved the library atmosphere and would get lost in the maze of books. His mother would often have to hunt him down when he hunkered down in one of the hundreds of shelf rows. Other than his adventures at the university, he grew up as most other boys and young men of his generation.

From early on he dreamed of going to the University. Entrance to the University was open to anyone meeting the scholastic requirements. Knowing this motivated him and he excelled in school. From his first years at the beginning, to his final lower-level education, he excelled through hard work but also because he had an exceptional mind. He was always at the top or near the top of his class.

He tested for the University and easily met the requirements.

His chosen field was the newly formed area of Astronomy. He took all the math and science courses required and was soon focused on the solar system and the stars.

Two things happened at Ulm that launched Raulens on his future path.

One was meeting the quiet but very beautiful woman of his dreams.

The second was his participation in the creation of a better telescope.

The beautiful woman of his dreams came first. She walked into the library where he was studying.

He looked up from where he was studying and knew immediately that he wanted to know her. He approached her and said hello.

Her black pupils and yellow eyes froze him on the spot. Her smile radiated warmth that he felt in his soul. He was left speechless. It seemed that he stared into her eyes for hours before he finally invited her out for a walk around the rim of the canyon.

To his surprise she accepted.

He would forever remember being overwhelmed each time she looked at him and smiled.

He knew he had met his soul mate and he managed to ask her name on that first meeting!

Milan was a good listener and from their first moment became his sounding board and occasional advisor. She never engaged directly in the discussion of theory or technical matters. She would periodically ask a clarifying question.

The questions were what Raulens loved. They seemed innocent and clueless, but they would always pull or push him in a new direction. He struggled to answer her questions in clear simple terms. Her questions were the magic elixir that activated his mind.

They were the icing on the cake or the sugar on his berries.

Soon Raulens came to realize how much in love he was with Milan. She was constantly on his mind, and he found himself talking to her even when they were not together.

He joked with her that her questions were even better when she wasn't around.

He asked her to become his mate. Her acceptance overjoyed him.

His parents were overjoyed. They also fell in love with Milan. They asked Raulens what he had done to be so lucky. He smiled and joked that he had to show Milan pictures of his parents to ensure her that he was suitable before she agreed to be his mate.

Overwhelming in its totality of the physical evidence, the physics and the astronomy convinced Raulens the universe randomly but continuously built and destroyed the stars and any Orbs traveling around these stars.

He and his colleagues postulated that their Orb had almost been destroyed by some huge space traveling object and the canyon where they all lived was a result of this collision. The canyon was a fracture of the surface mantle.

Their model had much of the original atmosphere being lost at the time of the collision.

Additionally, the impact had been so powerful and deep that it most likely distorted the core and created an imbalance of the magnetic field of the planet. This in turn allowed the radiation from the sun to stream in through holes in the magnetic field that was now more like a roof that the wind had ripped some covering off and allowed the sun's rays to come through in an unfiltered way.

He was not religious, but he believed in miracles.

It was a miracle that life on the Orb had evolved at all.

It was a miracle that there was sufficient oxygen left to sustain life.

It was a miracle that sentient beings had survived in the radiation rich environment.

His enthusiasm for learning was complemented with a tenacious need to create.

When he took basic astronomy, he was disappointed by the lack of clarity of the telescopes pointed at the night sky. He could see the stars very clearly with his own eyes but saw larger but distorted blobs of light through the telescopes. The available telescopes at the university made the stars larger but fuzzy and disoriented. It was hard to learn anything from what he saw.

He preferred to use his direct eyesight to learn about the lights in the night sky.

He and his lifelong friend Pandl, an electronics specialist, began to study and develop a better way to make the lenses for the telescope. They pioneered a new way of making the lenses in pressurized chambers under the canyon waters. They were able to get a ten-fold increase in lens size and clarity

The design changes he made to the telescope and the new lenses he developed dramatically increased what and how far the telescopes could see.

The more than tenfold improved clarity was a huge breakthrough.

Pandl went on to invent light amplification technology that digitized the visual information and created a computer image. This allowed for the refined correction of the light being focused.

Once again, a dramatic breakthrough was achieved.

Together the two guided the building of the current telescope and control system housed in the Observatory. They had been the key designers of the concept of raising the telescope at night and retracting it during the day.

The protective water filled seal had been another concept that they had initiated. This allowed the telescope to escape the destructive radiation from the sun during daylight hours.

Their improvements and their subsequent work in the field leapfrogged the knowledge of the Orb System.

The clarity provided by the telescope lens allowed Raulens to discover eight Orbs traveling around the central star.

This revolutionized the understanding of their system.

This elevated the standing of both he and Pandl to where they manage a huge budget of their own.

Subsequent discoveries and calculation proved their central star and its orbs traveled around yet another center. This center was not visible with their current technology but what they could see with their telescopes allowed them to postulate the mathematics of this grand central point.

The improved telescopes allowed Raulens to see and become mesmerized with the third orb from the sun. It seemed rich in oxygen and in water. It seemed alive. He wanted desperately to see it up close.

His achievements, his fame, and his home life combined to make Raulens a person that was empowered and motivated.

He knew he was rich in everything that mattered.

Family life took Raulens on another journey of discovery. He was overjoyed when Milan announced she was pregnant. He put as much energy into the planning for his family as he had done in the field of astronomy.

First, he found a home to be only for he and Milan. This meant that both of them moved away from their families into their own home.

This was rare in the Orb's society, but he knew that he wanted to be closer to his work than either of their parents did.

As a professor at the University, Raulens was able to gain access to a small but very comfortable habitat just a short distance away from the main campus. It was a lucky break for him. He was still too junior to rate these specific accommodations but no one else was seeking them.

Lamens approved as soon as she walked through the habitat. It was relatively humble, but it felt right.

Raulens spent all his extra time making the habitat a place that he and Lamens could call their home. He wanted a place where their child or children could grow and develop. Their habitat soon became a refuge for both of them.

Both of them were leading developers and inventors in their field. Their energy went into both their personal work in their fields and into making their home life a focal point.

They both worked a great deal of time from a joint office in their home.

Kerin, his first born, was almost a duplicate of himself. He was a serious young cub but one that loved to be with the two of them.

The birth of his son brought new meaning to the work Raulens was doing. Raulens doubled down on his studies and writings about the condition of their Orb and the study of the space around the Orb. He was now thinking into the future of his son. He spent a great deal of time with his son and many of his traits transferred to the young cub.

His consistent accomplishments over the years moved him up in his field. He quickly went up the academic levels and became the Dean of Astronomy. This allowed him to continue his study of the orbital system.

He scoured the night sky and found multiple objects that he wrote about and illustrated.

Two sun cycles later, Lamens once again announce her pregnancy.

He made sure to clear the second child with the Orb's agency that managed such matters. His status earned him their approval.

This time it was a girl.

Raulens knew from the moment he saw her that she was special. Her eyes were yellow and black like her mother's, but they had a deeper more mysterious depth. The first time Nadia looked into his eyes he knew there was a deep bond between them. He could feel her in his mind and in his soul.

The future of his two children became the driver for his search for an alternate world for the Orb's population. Such a quest was now more personal and closer to home.

He once again poured over all the learning he had done to date and planned ahead to even more detailed studies of their solar neighborhood. He wanted to provide a way to escape his fractured Orb and locate to a rich and whole one.

The fragile condition and the situation on his Home Orb made Raulens look out to see if there was another orb that could provide a home for his people.

It was during a new study of the Orbs and using yet another enhancement of his telescope that Raulens made another discovery that would become his obsession.

The third Orb from the central star appeared to have life!

His analysis of the light spectrum being reflected by this orb confirmed what his eyes saw looking into the telescope. The Orb was oxygen rich. It was over eighty percent water with what appeared to be a huge land mass. The evidence of abundant life was overwhelming.

The type of life and whether it was intelligent in the same way as he, was the central question needing an answer?

The orb was a blue, white, and green gem in the heavens.

He spent several cycles convincing himself of his conclusions. During this time, he would take Nadia with him to the observatory. After the setting of the sun, the two of them would walk the path along the top of the canyon. He would point out the constellations and tell Nadia stories about the different groups. These were stories he made up to entertain Nadia, but he used his stories in his writings about the various stars. The stories became popular throughout the Orb and eventually textbooks.

His astronomy textbooks were used in all the other universities as well as at Ulm.

Periodically Keren would accompany him as well. Keren was more interested in the biological plant work Lamens was doing and would more often be with her.

The discovery and the realization that there seemed to be life on the third orb changed the course of his career.

He had swiftly risen to the leadership of the Astronomy Department at Ulm. He had been in this role for five cycles.

It took him another three cycles to convince the Orb leaders to fund the program he proposed to develop the technology to support the exploration of the third orb.

Raulens put all his energy into establishing and getting the funding for the development of space travel. This was a rather long and tedious effort that entailed convincing allies and in some political arm twisting and deal making with those on the other side of the issue.

Educating key leaders to the rapidly decaying atmosphere of the Orb proved to be the most powerful means of reaching an agreement that moved their funding request forward. Finally, after almost a full cycle of struggle, the resources needed to build a new space complex was appropriated.

This was a huge victory, but it also offered another source of employment for a growing population, and it provided the means of extracting a large amount of materials from under the mantel.

He and Pandl pioneered the development of the rockets needed to get out to space. They spent two cycles designing and testing a series of rockets. They launched two orbiting telescopes as part of testing their rockets.

The in space telescopes provided an immediate improvement of the ability to see even farther out into the space around them.

The success of the telescope launches solidified the support and the continued funding of their efforts.

Raulens now had the leverage he had sought. He obtained enough support to get a large facility designed and built to house their space program.

Raulens was out on the newly developed space exploration site located one hundred ticks away from the edge of Ulm. The site, like all other facilities, was mostly underground. The rocket launch sites were round tubes bored down into the ground and designed with a heavy cover similar to the one shielding the telescope at Ulm. This protected those inside the tube. It allowed the building of or maintaining a rocket in a radiation free area.

The site had six launch tubes. These were built in a straight line.

The maintenance facilities were built along each side at the base of the tubes.

The labs and other manufacturing and assembly facilities were built farther underground on both sides of the launch tubes below the maintenance facilities

He and Pandl had been directly involved in the design and building of the space exploration center. The site was now fully operational and staffed with over twenty thousand personnel. The possibility of colonizing the third Orb had been taken seriously and the funding to build the facility went through the council in relatively smooth fashion.

It was actually supported by both the believers of the program and those who thought it would never pan out. The non-believers saw it as a major source of new jobs that were needed to boost the economy.

A site located well away from Ulm had been chosen for safety reasons. Several of the rockets tested by Raulens and Pandl had exploded on their launch pads or shortly after launch.

After seven orb cycles the construction was complete and the site was fully functional.

Raulens was studying the schematic of his latest rocket design. These were the blueprints and plans for a rocket designed to travel to the third orb. Launching and propelling the rocket was a challenge the team had easily overcome.

The remaining obstacle was to provide adequate radiation protection for those in the rockets. And it was a monumental and so far, unsolved issue. To date only a partial solution had been developed. Shielding could easily be achieved. But the weight of a water shielded rocket made it impossible to lift it into space. They did not have the engines with enough power to provide such enormous lift.

Raulens divided his time between rocket engine design and the continuing study of the third Orb.

Since the third Orb was much closer to the sun and was exposed to a higher density of radiation, his current theory was that it was shielded from the significantly more intense radiation by a robust magnetic field. Raulens' calculated that the radiation level hitting the third Orb was at least forty percent more intense than hitting his Home Orb.

He then determined the magnetic field had to be at least twice as strong as the one on his Home Orb. When he put this all together, he postulated that magnetic field strength was proportional to the shielding it provided.

Raulens sent several teams out to gather data to prove this thesis. They gathered radiation data around his Home Orb. The Home Orb radiation field was well mapped, and the strong areas and the distorted areas were known. Field measurements taken around the orb verified the theory.

He made two additional and very discouraging breakthroughs.

The apparent gravity of the third Orb was almost twice as much as his own Orb. Refined measurements and calculations utilizing the interaction of the huge moon of the third orb put the exact gravitational pull at two point six that of his Home Orb.

This significantly higher gravitational force significantly decreased the possibility of directly colonizing the third Orb. This meant the explorer would need to withstand this dramatically greater force. These forces were well beyond what any Orbian could experience directly and live.

Exoskeletons were designed to overcome the physical strength required for movement on the third orb. These exoskeletons became an immediate success and were being deployed by his son Keren in the mantel tunneling projects.

They were excellent at giving individuals extra work capacity. This resulted in a speed up of the tunneling work.

Keren's use of the exoskeletons also made the improvements of them faster and more economical.

There use was broadly advertised to show that the space program was resulting in immediately useful technology and was paying for itself.

However, the more complicated issue with populating the third orb was the stress the additional gravity would have on the internal organs of the Orbians. Testing on the ability of the organs to continue to function properly was currently under way.

The most successful approach was for the individual to be totally submerged in a liquid. This meant the individual needed to acclimate to use an incompressible liquid with which to breathe instead of just air. It was difficult to acclimate to this environment.

This was the same technology the deep-sea colonies were experimenting with. The fifty candidates for this program were all practicing with this approach. This solution would allow exploration excursions to the third orb, but it would not support long term colonization.

This fact was a huge disappointment to Raulens. He had hoped to open up another orb into which their total population could expand.

The increase in radiation as one went toward the blue Orb was another huge barrier. A rocket traveling in toward the third orb would experience a radiation increase proportional to the square of the distance traveled toward the sun. This he realized was monumental.

Current technology did not have a way to overcome the radiation threat. Radiation shielding capable of shielding the Orbian needed to be designed into the rockets.

Very dense materials helped greatly but those were rare on the Orb. Water was effective to a degree, but this too was a very precious resource, and it would limit the size of the rocket and number of Orbians able to make such a trip.

The quantities of all the materials required to make a safe environment was a huge barrier.

Launching the required amount of material into space was next to impossible. His team needed to come up with some material providing superior shielding but light enough to easily and economically be put into space.

The current focus was the development of a material capable of actively absorbing the radiation and converting it into useable energy. The goal was to develop a thin membrane that could cover the exterior of the spaceship. Currently the material in the lab was a one-use material that then became inert. What was needed was a material that consistently and continuously converted the incoming radiation into useful energy.

Currently there was an effort underway to measure the radiation intensity more precisely. The whole endeavor pivoted on the success and information of the unattended probes. These probes had been launched and were beginning to send back the radiation data that would allow for a more precise understanding.

There was no question that the challenge of getting to the third orb was monumental. The combination of the radiation and the physical challenges of higher gravitational pull put a visit to the third orb many cycles away. It was perhaps a lifetime away.

Raulens took it hard, but he continued the learning and expanded his field of search out away from their Grand Orb.

Six unattended rockets were planned.

Two rockets were complete and already on their way.

They would serve two purposes.

One they would provide specific radiation level measurement between the two planets. Second, they would provide planetary data as they closed in on and finally entered the atmosphere of the third orb. This planetary data would provide final confirmation of the conditions and the status of life on the blue orb.

Raulens was in the middle of his current project focus.

The work on the development of a more effective radiation shield utilizing lead, gold and water vanished from his mind when he received Nadia's call for help.

From little on it was clear to Raulens that Nadia was special. Her mental capacity far exceeded his. She had been number one in all her classes before going to Ulm. She remained number one for her entire scholastic career.

Upon graduation Nadia had chosen to follow in his footsteps. Nadia had risen in the ranks of the Astronomy Department even faster than he. She had a continuous stream of discoveries of the space around them. She had edited several of his writings and improved several of the observations he and his colleagues had made. She credited this with the continuing improvement of the telescopes and the addition of the orbiting ones, but he saw that she had also made adjustments to the mathematical model equations.

He took her comments of that of a loving daughter not wanting to disturb her old man.

They saw each other often when Raulens went to the observatory to study the third Orb. The fact that she had asked him for help meant she was worried about some new find.

He listened to her explanation of why she was calling. He immediately left his office and went to the observatory. Nadia had either found a new and seemingly threatening anomaly or Nadia had made a monumental error. Nadia was such a thorough person that the second consideration was only momentary. Raulens turned his thoughts to what the unknown anomaly might be. In either case he needed to examine the situation firsthand.

Raulens took the underground tube to the elevator that led to the surface. He was going to walk the path that he had so often taken to the observatory. He wanted to look up into the sky and see the stars.

He was surprised when he exited on the surface and was greeted by Nadia. Her smile and hug warmed his soul. She had anticipated his approach and had come out to greet him and hand in hand take their walk together.

Chapter 3: Milan

Milan was a product of the farm country. Her family had spent generations building and improving the many farm terraces that graced the canyon. She had grown up hiking up and down these terraces. She had chased the small furry animal known to all as a quizl.

The quizl was the only other land creature on the Orb. She and the quizl were friends. She would often sit on the terrace walls and hand feed them. They came in three colors just like the people of the orb. There were the light tan ones, the darker brown ones, and the black ones. They were all shy and usually stayed in their burrows when the farm workers were around. Milan was one of the few Orbians that these creatures seemed to accept.

Though the Orbians were family oriented and normally preferred to be in the company of others, Milan would be what you would call a loner. She loved to wander the terraces by herself. She took in the details of the terraces and noted flaws that had been overlooked.

She made improvement suggestions to specific farm teams and soon became known to many of them as the "inspector" because of her keen eye for details.

Milan learned firsthand what the farmers did to make things grow. She learned about the planting process, the fertilization and then the tending. She enjoyed her work in the field. She was a farm girl. Her heart was in planting the seed and then nurturing the plant to give the greatest yield. Each season she would grow some specific plant on her own.

Her mother encouraged her to learn more. Early on the family went on a visit to the University to expose Milan to the many fields in the Agricultural Development Department. This was a turning point for the young cub. She immediately began to dream of improving what she saw in the fields. She began to read the many books of plants and farming. She found many inconsistencies and counter points of view. She took notes and started a journal of her own observations and conclusions.

She did not anticipate that her journal would later be published in the form of a reference on plants.

She excelled in her schoolwork and a few cycles later she applied and was accepted to Ulm University.

She attended Ulm University in order to increase her ability to make the improvements she dreamed of making out on the terraced canyon farmlands.

Her intellect and curiosity provided her with constant new ideas in the field of biology where she could make improvements. She learned how to channel certain plant traits to make these desired improvements. She also successfully experimented in creating totally new strains of plants.

Unaware of her beauty she was surprised at what seemed to be a constant assault on her by her male counterparts. She handled this by staying away from the student parties and spending time secluded in the various libraries around the campus.

It was on one of her many trips into the main campus library where she met her mate.

She was in the middle of researching the history of a specific melon when she heard a squeaky, "Hello."

She turned and had to look slightly down at a rather handsome young man with almost grey eyes. He seemed rather awkward as he stood and tried to start a conversation with her. She stood silently and just smiled at him.

She had come to realize that her tall slender appearance, sandy fuzz, and her nearly yellow eyes made her a magnet for the young men at Ulm. She normally easily dismissed them with a cold reply.

This one seemed different. He was awkward but determined. He stared at her with his grey eyes and seemed to look deep inside her.

She felt him immediately at her soul level.

"I would like to know you better. Will you walk the canyon rim with me this evening and enjoy the light of the many stars?" was his request.

This was not what Milan had expected. All other advances came with an invitation to dinner, a dance, or a theatrical presentation. They were invitations trying to show how capable the inviter was.

This invitation was a humble one that had a totally different slant.

She thought about this for a moment. She accepted the invitation. She was curious about this walk.

At the time of acceptance, she did not know it would be a walk she would never forget.

It opened up a totally new world of the Orb to her. Everything about the subsequent relationship was refreshing to Milan.

There was always a new twist or unexpected occurrence.

Raulens, she found out was brilliant and constantly challenging himself and others around him to do more, to get better.

This infected her thinking as well. She was energized by his presence. She could also feel his intensity.

She knew immediately that she could not follow his scientific discussions and explanations of his detailed work. She constantly threw out her questions in hopes of at least learning the basics. This turned out to be the right approach. Her questions seemed to encourage Raulens.

He in turn asked her questions about her plant development ideas.

"Why do plants need light to grow? Could you make a plant that grows in the dark? How fast could you make a plant grow?" were some of the questions he posed.

Then came the question she had been waiting for. When Raulens proposed to her, there was no question to her acceptance. She had come to realize he was her mate long before his proposal. She had chosen to let proposal to come in its own time.

When it came, she felt her world become complete.

Both of them graduated at the same time.

They each went on the specialty each was passionate about.

He continued to make amazing progress in his field.

She continually created variations of the plants she worked with and significantly increased farm production.

She gave birth to Keren the following cycle. She instantly saw Raulens as she held her newly born put in her arms. He was a quiet baby and seemed content when he was either with her or Raulens.

Two cycles later, Nadia was born. She had much the same eye coloring as herself, but her eyes were even more distinct. Nadia was an intense cub. She was soon the dominant child. She grew taller than her brother. He was broad and more muscular, while Nadia was tall and slender.

The two got along exceedingly well and it was clear that Keren adored his sister and looked out for her.

The population on the Orb was a controlled one. Two offspring was the limit allowed for their family. A third would be possible if the quota that was analyzed each year took a shifted upward. Any change was based on increasing the food production from the limited farm area.

Children were precious. Everyone looked out for the young.

Milan took the two with her everywhere she went. She was constantly out in the fields continuing her work in improving the yield of the farmlands. The two scurried after her as she examined the various plant conditions.

Soon it became clear that Nadia loved to go with Raulens. She was spending more time with him. For a time both Keren and Nadia spent more time with Raulens than with her. She wondered what Raulens was doing that attracted them.

Many cycles later she learned about the stories Raulens told them about the sparkling lights in the dark night sky as the three walked the canyon rim. This had been the main attraction.

She missed them but knew that they would gravitate to what interested them more.

When their formal training began there was once again a shift with whom they spent their time with.

Keren gravitated to spending time with her both in her lab and out in the field.

Nadia clearly was hooked on being with Raulens and studying the stars.

Milan noted that a quizl family had established themselves in the new terrace wall. In the many cycles that she had been out on the terraces she came to realize that the quizl seemed to be flourishing. Her curiosity made her go look in the library at Ulm for information about the quizl.

"Do you realize that the last book about the quizl is more than twenty cycle old," she had commented to the family as they share one of their dinners.

"Well, what do the quizl do but eat some of the food we grow?" Nadia commented.

"They are cute and fun to watch. There seem to be a lot of them. I wonder how many there are?" Keren added.

"I think we should make it a Namens family project to write a book about the population, the habits, the number and the contribution of the quizl," Raulens suggested.

And so, the family began to gather information about the quizl. They sent out a questionnaire to the terrace farm workers to get a count of the furry animals. They also asked about the habits and action of the quizl.

"There seem to be almost as many quizl as there are Orbians," Nadia noted as she and Keren tallied the returns of the questionnaires.

"They may actually be helping by pollinating the flowers of our plants," Milan commented as she read the information send in by the various farm teams.

"Let's focus our next family outing on closely following the actions of a specific quizl family," Raulens suggested.

"I have just the family of quizl for us to study. I have had one quizl family that I have followed since I was a young girl. I know them and they know me. I know that their life span is about half of ours. I have just met the new offspring of the third generation," Milan shared with the rest.

And so, the family studied Milan's quizl family. They learned that the quizl were pollinating the plants. This was an amazing discovery for Milan. In all the years in agriculture she had not thought about how the plants were reproducing. How could she have overlooked the obvious?

The book, *"The Quizl, Our Partners"* by the Namens Family was published a cycle later. Each of the family had written some specific chapter and Raulens had provided the overall editing.

"We now have a family book to be proud of," Milan commented as she put the book out on the main entrance table.

Not only was the book on the coffee table but it ended up being one of the key books used in all schools on the Orb.

Milan continually provided agricultural changes leading to increases in the production of food. To say she had green digits was an understatement. Her breakthrough developments made her the most prolific agricultural engineer in Orbian history. She became better known on the Orb than Raulens. Her success meant an immediate easier life for the Orbians.

Her current project was the development of plants able to grow in totally artificial and very dim light.

"Yes, it was Raulens' questions that has brought me to this point, but it is my work that is giving the answers," Milan thought to herself.

Her new nutritious mushrooms could flourish in underground green houses with the minimum energy use.

The Home Orb had ample surface space but few remaining habitable areas. The outer surfaces of the Orb were uninhabitable because of the high radiation from the sun.

The current population was at its ultimate peak unless new regions could be opened. Advances in medicine and more abundant resources contributed to longer life spans. Even with the strict population control laws, the count was slowly creeping upward.

This was a current political issue for those elected to govern.

The success of Milan's projects coupled with the ones focused on the creation of water would open extensive under mantel living areas.

This in turn would allow the population to expand into giant tunnels being carved through the mantel.

Expansion into new areas was of great interest.

One group of scientist started several underwater colonies. However, few of the population could envision having an underwater life.

The more serious focus was on farming fish and cultivating several sea plants. The sea plants had high nutritional value. The success of increasing the quantity of the sea plants and advertising how to add them into salads and other foods was making them popular across the Orb.

Most Orbians only ate plant life-based foods. A few were willing to eat fish. Fish was popular but the quantity was not sufficient to make it a significant food source. It remained an exotic dish. This was seen as a promising area but one taking decades to expand and to make any significant impact.

The more promising endeavor was the tunneling taking place to create highways under the planet's surface. This allowed expansion into the huge expanse of the mantel. The problem was tunneling cost and timing. Tunneling was slow and expensive.

The tunneling did have the benefit of extracting many of the minerals and raw materials needed by industry. This duel potential and value was the equation supporting the current extensive tunneling effort. The tunneling project received the greatest funding and was making good headway.

The expansion of the gardens was another positive side product from the tunneling effort. Milan was following the tunneling work closely because it yielded a tremendous amount of soil. She worked with the engineers to process and use the more nutrient materials from the tunneling to create terraces up the side of the steep canyon walls. These terraces were being turned into additional garden and farming areas.

Milan was very specific as to the specification of the soil that was to be processed for the farming areas.   The tunnel borers also called her the "inspector" because she was constantly testing the soil mix being sent out to the terraces.

The less useful stone and other materials were used to raise the top edges of the canyon walls to create additional day time radiation shielding for the canyon. It was an effective way to dispose of the large quantities of the tunnel materials. The rise in the canyon height yielded a few more feet of growing space on the terraces built up on the far side of the canyon. A ten percent increase in production was a very significant increase.

One work cycle, Milan was out on a newly created farm terrace level. She was inspecting one of the many test plots she cultivated. She looked down to the terraces below her and across the valley to the opposite side.

She was several hundred levels up and had a clear view across the canyon. She estimated she was up at least to the commercial level of the city.

Each level had openings looking out into the canyon. These openings were made of leaded glass. Those walking from business to business enjoyed a panoramic view of the valley. Some exclusive apartments were also built with this external view. Milan lost count of the hundreds of levels rising up from the floor of the canyon toward the top.

Her own home was well back toward the upper center of the city. She knew that just on her financial credits the family could afford to live in one of the exclusive exterior apartments, but she loved their small cozy home. She knew Raulens felt the same way.

Her gaze came back to the base of the terrace farm plots. The radiation shield at the top of the canyon had reached a new height. The additional shielding allowed this new terrace to be added.

On this specific plot she was growing a succulent water laden yellow melon. The melons for which she had received Orbian wide recognition were now close to full size.

They proved to be hearty, radiation resistant plants. They were designed to withstand the higher level of radiation to which they were exposed on this terrace. Their success would increase the growing capacity of the canyon.

Milan walked slowly back to the transit system. Her eyes naturally examined the condition of the terrace wall as she was walking by. She was pleased to see a quizl family had established a home in the wall of the new terrace. She hoped they would do a thorough job in pollinating her new plants.

A host of workers were waiting for the tram back to the base of the city. Most of the farm workers split their time between the day and the night cycle. The daylight portion of the work cycle allowed for the inspection and maintenance of the terraces. The cultivation work requiring the majority of the workers was done after sunset to ensure the lowest radiation exposure to the greatest number of workers. The trams were conveniently located and separated by only fifteen ticks from each other. There were hundreds of cross canyon trams. This made the trip to each of the terraces a simple journey.

The ride back took Milan past a variety of food, fiber and chemical producing terraces and growing plots. All current plants and legumes had been heavily engineered. They were designed to provide the necessary starches, proteins, and chemicals needed for sustenance. Special grasses and vines also provided the fiber to make garments, furniture, and structural building materials.

Milan was amazed that when saturated with certain resins and put under great pressure certain fibers generated amazing structural strength. The grain of these materials was in themselves appealing and beautiful.

It would take her a full hundred ticks to get back to her laboratory. She relaxed and looked down toward the opening of the canyon. The walls first went outward to their widest point. Then the walls of the canyons seemed to come together and close. Milan knew this was an optical illusion. The walls of the canyon continued for several thousand ticks before a sea of water met the floor of the valley. Then the waters continued on almost half the way around the orb.

"Our orb is like the melon I dropped from the counter," she thought as she arrived at her destination.

She proceeded to her lab where she was working on a new strain of legumes. These would be able to grow in almost virtual darkness. This was an important development in support of colonies to be built totally underground. She hoped to make a breakthrough on extending the capability of these plants to grow in low light levels and to generate a high nutritional value.

Raulens had called to let her know he was going to meet Nadia in her observatory office. He would bring Nadia home for the morning meal.

Milan decided to feature some of her new plants and legumes.

Chapter 4: Keren

Keren, Nadia's older brother, looked a lot like his father but had more slender build and was a bit taller. He had the same grey eyes and matching grey fuzz. Quietly handsome and in great shape, he had many of the eligible ladies after him. He however was not a lady's man. He had a more serious and focused nature about him. It was clear he had a specific purpose and exuded confidence in the way he commanded attention when he entered a room.

From little on he had been inquisitive and focused. Once he focused on some concept or idea, he would pursue it until it yielded the information, knowledge, or the result he sought.

He was also a controller. The information he sought was usually to be used to control or influence some situation or to create a specific desired outcome. From little on he learned to influence and guide those around him. He had a good heart, and he followed the guidance of the principles his mother and father taught him.

His actions were not about taking advantage of people but almost exactly the opposite. He sought to create situations where everyone was treated equally.

He did not have his mother's passion for plants and farming. He did not have his father's passion for the stars and the orbs around the central Orb.

His passion was the expansion in the number of Orbians. He wanted their number to expand. He had no grand scheme or insight only a deep resolve.

He had entered Ulm University because he could, and his family pushed him to do so. He, however, did not have a specific area of interest. He went looking for what might interest him. He found it in the pursuit of a political science degree. The nuances of politically influencing, guiding, and creating the rules for the Orbian society intrigued him.

He volunteered for one of the expansionist political leader's election campaigns. He wrote speeches and position papers for the campaign. These writings became central to the election effort. The Expansionist Party leaders took note of Keren and suggested he run for a position on the Ulm Orb Council.

"I have been asked to make a run for a position on the Ulm Orb Council by the Expansionist Party," Keren announced at one of the family meetings.

"That sounds like a great idea," Nadia said enthusiastically.

"Well, I think you getting into politics is a great idea but are you really for the idea of expanding our population?" Raulens asked.

"I am for the expansion of our living space by excavating our mantle. Once we have the living space, population expansion is a no brainer," Keren replied.

"That makes sense to me," Milan said as she took note of Keren's serious response.

She was sure this was her young man getting into some life-long effort that he would end up controlling and guiding.

"I will come to work for your election team," Nadia volunteered.

She was pleased to see Keren find a path that would harness his skills and passion to serve and improve the Orbian society.

Keren had Nadia to thank for much of his success. Nadia's fame as a singer and the songs she wrote on behalf of his campaign were instrumental in getting him elected. Her good looks and popularity as a world-famous singer made her a great spokesperson. She gave speeches on the concept of expansion of living space for the expansion of the Orbian population and in writing songs for his campaign. She would have been the one elected had she been running.

During Keren's election campaign they both made all the news broadcasts throughout the Orb. Because of their physical differences many who saw them together did not realize they were brother and sister. Nadia wrote and sang several songs about population expansion and the growth of the Mantel communities. These became big hits and resulted in huge support for Keren.

He won his election by a landslide.

He was currently a junior representative in the main house of the Ulm Orb Council (UOC). His active pursuit of the rights of the individual and his push for the expansion of living space and additional population growth made him very popular among the majority of Orbians.

It also made him unpopular with many of those traditionalists in the established power structure who were focused on population control. This was a sign to Keren that he was taking the right actions.

He pursued the reasons for the traditionalist's resistance to population expansion. It came down to two elements, the fear that there would not be enough food and the fear that there was not enough space.

"Well, my mother is working on their being enough food, so I will work on making enough space," Keren thought to himself.

For as long as Keren could remember, he had enjoyed the strong support of his family. He had never considered himself as capable as his father nor as inventive as his mother.

Nadia was the little sister he loved and to him she seemed to be a very talented genius. He knew she was brilliant and was probably the smartest one in the family.

She was now almost a foot taller than he. None the less he thought of her as his little sister and felt protective of her.

Her singing abilities made her one of the most popular figures on the Orb. Keren knew that his election had been helped greatly by the songs Nadia had written and sung for his campaign.

"I guess now it is my little sister that is 'looking out' for me," he thought to himself as he felt an inner warmth.

When the family was together it was always a pleasure when Nadia could be heard singing somewhere in the house. Keren always stopped to listen and admire the melodic pure timber of her voice. He had every recording of her music and listened to her on a daily basis.

Following his mother through the terraces and playing with Nadia among the various plants being studied, influenced Keren in subtle ways. He became focused on improving the lives of those around him. He wanted to see his race expand and grow. It was clear to him that the Orbian's current limitations needed to be overcome.

There had to be a way to change the world. He became determined to become that change agent.

He was amazed at the small overall area that the Orbians existed in. They needed more space. But the deadly radiation of the sun made most of their orb un-inhabitable.

There were strict population control laws regulating the population number. The strongly enforced one was the one for one replacement policy. It only allowed for another birth when there as a death. This was currently under heavy debate. Over centuries, the population had been managed to ensure a balance between, the old, middle, and young. It was roughly in balance.

Any territorial expansion was closely supervised. The goal was to maintain the current population but provide more space and resources. Later, a rise in the population would be considered. The debate was about the timing of any changes to this long maintained and strictly enforced law.

Keren was convinced the government needed to focus on leveraging the planetary resources to support a larger population. The planet provided plenty of space and resources for a larger population. The problem the population faced was making those resources and the space accessible. His main ambition was to expand the rail systems outward from each of the major canyons. He envisioned an expansion opening up tunnels leading to community centers in the mantel all the way around the Orb. He saw this as the opening of a wide frontier allowing for the doubling or the tripling of the world's current population.

His supporters were in the majority. He leveraged this support to move into a position where he could take ever more effective action. He was a tough negotiator and won most of his positions by the application of logic and the application of pressure by whatever means he could wield it.

His influence on the council was much higher than any other junior member. This was mostly due to his own efforts but his family name and the success of all his family members often proved of great assistance. He had leveraged all of his family members as he navigated the bumpy road of the political environment.

He became the primary force behind the tunneling projects. He co-authored and helped pass the Tunneling Act aimed at the expansion of livable space. The act set a goal to establish an in the mantel community of a million families in the next five cycles.

The tunneling was currently in full progress. The primary tunneling project was located halfway between Ulm and New Ulm. The main connection tunnel went away from the rail tunnel at a ninety-degree angle. This branch would go out for one hundred clicks. Later it would continue until one day it made its way totally around the Orb.

He envisioned this first circumvention as the first of thousands more. The tunneling would continue through the lives of hundreds of Orbian tunnel diggers.

The excavations to each side of the tunnel would create large chambers. Each chamber would be able to house multiple families or hold small businesses.

The community design would follow the layout already in used in all the orb living areas. The initial level would be the level for food production. This is where Milan's low light level plants would add their value.

Keren suggested the development of low light level fiber producing plants. These could then be used to produce construction materials.

Above the food production area would be the factory level and farther up would be the living area. Keren joked he would establish the Namens University at the top level.

The success of the first tunneling effort led to Keren managing the tunnel building out to the new space center. This in turn put him in contact with all the new inventions as that the space program was developing.

The exoskeleton development to explore the third Orb was a huge break through. Raulens had shown Keren this invention. Keren had immediately asked for a hundred to be made for his tunneling team. These exoskeletons were a huge success and greatly increased the speed of tunnel construction.

The tunnel for the new space center was completed in record time. Keren also used the boring machines made to create the spaceship launch tubes to create similar but smaller vertical tubes for huge elevator shafts. These tubes were then sealed at the top with an in expensive mix of soil and water that once dry formed a new radiation covering of these tunnels.

A new community capable of housing ten million Orbians came into existence in record time. The excavation to expand this area would continue for many foreseeable cycles.

His re-election in the coming campaign was considered a certainty. He was rapidly acquiring more political influence and was selected to lead the prominent Ulm Council finance committee. This achievement put him on the council leadership committee and in a position to influence a wide variety of pending legislation.

He knew he had achieved getting to the position of considerable influence. He was personally pleased, but he considered it a good beginning and looked forward to making more happen.

Political pundits saw Keren as a very likely candidate to be the Orb Council Leader in the coming years. It was a position most said was his to lose.

Keren had no intentions of losing. He planned to follow his passion of making a significant difference to the wellbeing of the Orbian community. He planned on continually renewing himself and keeping current on what was happening to the world around him.

<u>Chapter 5: Nadia's Discovery</u>

Three major telescopes orbited the planet. They had been designed, launched, and utilized as part of Raulens' program to study the third Orb. The position and the clarity of the images from these three space faring telescopes exceeded those on the ground. They had the latest advances in both the lenses they utilized and in the electronics that digitized the images. They provided exceptional views of the entire Orb system and the stars beyond.

The ability to point them at the various areas of interest made them especially useful. The added clarity of their vision made discovery a continuous event at all the facilities utilizing them. Every moment of every study was shared with all the universities. These studies were submitted to a council that allocated time based on the evaluation of the study.

Nadia had the most control because of her early comprehensive project proposals. She had submitted a proposal to track close flyby objects, a proposal to map the path of all the objects traveling around the Central Orb, and to map their position relative to each other. These projects were broad enough that they allowed for additional studies and learning for various sub projects. Nadia's main projects were followed and contributed to by all the universities and their teams.

Each member of Nadia's team was assigned to interface with one of the other university teams to review their learning and to coordinate her team learning with the entire university community. This relationship among the various teams accelerated the learning of all the teams.

Support for her projects was strong and unwavering.

The ground-based telescopes at Ulm, New Ulm and Hueval continued to provide fundamental and excellent information. Together the satellite and ground telescopes made for a solid research system. Those programs looking outward to the stars were well supported and excelling in their knowledge development.

All the major orbs of the central Orb had been identified. The only argument was the size and nature of the eight orbs. Did they all have magnetic fields? Could they support life? Was there any other intelligent life on any of these satellites? The distances made the seeing and study of the orbs a challenge.

The continuing improvements in the production of the telescope lenses and the digitizing electronics contributed greatly to providing the means to answer many of these questions.

Nadia thought it would only be a matter of time for the Orbians to become masters of the Grand Orb system.

At the beginning of the work cycle Nadia gathered her team to share her current concern and worry.

"I have been following three distant objects that have been traveling toward our orb. They have mysteriously changed course. They changed course in unison. I have either discovered huge alien powered spaceships or some immeasurably strong mysterious force," Nadia stated.

"I want all of you to review my analysis and report your conclusions back to me," Nadia continued.

"Should we get the other observatories to take a look and let us know their learning," one of the team members inquired.

"Yes, that would be a great idea. Ask them to look back at their recorded data and see if they captured these objects on any of their earlier recordings," Nadia agreed.

"I am going to concentrate on the area ahead of where these objects are traveling. Let me know when you are done or get me if you have any questions," Nadia closed as she took her seat at her computer.

The review effort continued for ten work cycles. Each cycle created additional tension and concern for Nadia. Every night cycle she would get an update on her team's progress.

On the tenth work cycle, as she slowly studied the path ahead, she almost missed the area where there seemed to be nothing. She had been noting the stars in the background and then nothing. She was so tired she thought she had dosed off. She retraced her viewing only to experience the same blank area. On her third scan, she noted the beginning of the blank area and then the end of it. She retraced her scan several more times.

There was a nothing area, a black void, attracting the objects!

She had discovered a new phenomenon. She had no explanation but immediately knew there was something of great mass in that specific location. She did some initial calculations and estimates as to the mass needed to create an attracting force necessary to turn the three objects she had been following. She could not believe her estimates. It was time to get her team into this.

"Where are you on the analysis of my initial finding?" Nadia opened her team meeting.

"We have reached the same conclusion that you postulated. Some great force has pulled them, or you have found alien space vessels traveling together," was the answer.

"Ok, now I want each of you to scan an area that I call the 'area of nothingness'," Nadia said as she introduced her next finding.

"Wow, what in the Orb is it," one of the team called out as he scanned the area.

They all wondered what it could be. They all commented that there was no known area like the one they were "not" seeing.

"Now team I want you to estimate the mass that object must have to exert the pull it is exerting on the three objects," Nadia instructed as she ended the meeting.

Nadia then called several physicist friends and asked them to do a similar initial estimate of the mass of the object. Three sun cycles later she was sure there was a new phenomenon of unbelievable strength attracting the three tracked objects.

"Well, I no longer have any doubts about our findings or the initial estimates as to the mass of the object. Now I have concerns about our Orbs interaction with this entity," Nadia said in her next meeting.

Nadia had been tracking the three objects because they were going to be close flybys to her Home Orb. This caused her to quickly estimate how close the Home Orb and this new force would come to each other.

Her initial findings heightened her concern and worry to an even higher level. This was something outside her comprehension.

"Now I want the team to verify the interaction of our Orb with this unknown entity," Nadia said in her next meeting.

Her team had confirmed her initial findings. It was the same with the additional findings. The team reiterated her concern.

"This is a threat to our entire population," one of the team members volunteered after discussing Nadia's analysis.

Nadia made a call to Raulens to ask for his help and guidance. At first, he thought she had made a mistake and told her to run through the analysis again. She explained she had done this more than a dozen times and each of her team members had separately confirmed the observation.

"I need your review before I share this more broadly with the outside world," Nadia replied.

"Let me come over and go through it firsthand," Raulens replied.

He needed to see the phenomenon and review the data himself. He could make no further suggestion until he got close to the data.

Nadia's team was in the middle of a heated round of discussion and postulating various theories about what the area of nothing might be when Raulens arrived.

Raulens first act was to visually observe the phenomenon in question.

"Please show me the three objects in question," was his first request.

The whole team suddenly understood where Nadia had picked up the quirk of looking into the telescope.

After a few moments of observation Raulens made his next request.

"Now show me the area of nothingness," he said quietly.

"Ok now on the screen show the entire journey in time lapse speed up," Raulens requested.

Later after the time lapse showing ended Raulens thank the team and requested all the data that had been accumulated and analysis associated with it. He let them know that he would analyze it and let them know his conclusions when he got through."

He spent the rest of the day going over the analysis of the path and the changes in the paths of the three objects. His review of the calculations confirmed what the team had found.

He found no errors.

He took the additional step of calculating the phenomenal gravitational attraction strength the black void exerted on the surrounding area to cause the objects to change course and be pulled toward it.

This calculation confirmed Nadia's earlier estimates.

Nadia then showed Raulens her initial projection of the interaction of the solar system and the new mysterious object. The phenomenon would pass through their region of space. It would come in toward their star very close to the path of their Orb.

"We need to do a thorough analysis as to whether any of the inner Orbs will be directly affected or interact with this object. Your team should develop a model of where each Orb will be when the solar system and this object come together.

We need to know in detail what happened to those three objects. Then we need to evaluate what our actions should be based on what is learned and how close we will come to the black void," Raulens told the team.

He displayed an outer calm but internally he was greatly alarmed. He now understood Nadia's request for help.

This was unchartered territory. It was a situation that no one had previously encountered.

Before he left, Raulens also contacted several of his colleagues to get them engaged and involved in the analysis.

Nadia looked around at her team and realized that Raulens had overwhelmed them.

"Well now you know how I feel when I am around my father," Nadia said jokingly.

Several of the team laughed.

"Yes, it was an overwhelming whirl wind, but I feel we measured up," another member tossed out.

"After all we have our own whirl wind, and she is as smart as her father."

"I have no doubts about my team members. You are among the best on the Orb. And as a team you are the best. Thank you," Nadia replied.

"Let's go home. Tomorrow we will put together a presentation to share for the Department and University Leadership. I will schedule meetings with our chairman and the rest.

We also need to do the analysis about our encounter with this unknown aberration," Nadia said as she closed the team meeting.

Nadia had not been fooled by her father's calm display. She could read him like a book.

He had been very alarmed and his immediate call to his friends confirmed the seriousness of the situation.

She now felt sure her own unease was justified. She left personally depressed

This would, she knew, become a very hot political issue.

She thought about the resources she needed to marshal to provide the information and data that would convince those in power to make a difference to take the appropriate action.

Politically, Keren made the top of the list.

She was surprised to learn that it was her lifelong friend, Lamins, was who she should call on to understand the position of all the various orbs.

She scheduled a series of meetings with the Ulm University leaders. First in line was her direct boss and department chairman. Next, she scheduled the science Department and finally the general Ulm University Leaders. She knew they would need to understand and participate in this important discovery and to support the analysis with time and resources.

Even though she stressed the importance of the meetings, other than her immediate department chairman, the meetings were all scheduled at least twenty work cycles into the future.

At first this disturbed her. Then she realized it gave her time to do a comprehensive study of the issues in question.

She got her team to collect all the data for as far back as they could. Then they did a comprehensive review of all events and occurrences for which they had data. This was a tedious analysis effort consuming all of their time.

"I want to build a comprehensive understanding of how this object might have interacted with our Orb system in the past and how it will interact with it in the near future," Nadia instructed her team.

She had reassigned the work for her team to be solely focused on this one issue.

She called and asked Lamins if he had the time to help her team and got his immediate support.

Little did she know that he had tried in every way to get as close to her as a possible. He ha chosen to develop his current expertise so he would have deep knowledge of the Grand Orbit system and even systems beyond.

The team's findings and Lamins model of the course the solar system and its interaction with the black void made all of Nadia's previous concerns minor. The void would pass through the solar system at almost the path of their Orb. The team was currently calculating exactly where in their cycle their Home Orb would be.

Nadia spent her time following the three objects and thinking through how the void and her Orb would interact.

On the fifteenth cycle after the discovery, the three asteroids arrived at the void. Nadia spent the next three days watching as the objects were drawn into the void and disappeared! This was an additional unparalleled and shockingly stunning learning. She repeatedly played back the event and viewed it in slow motion. Each object seemed to accelerate as it got closer to the black void. Then suddenly there was a flash of light and then nothing!

"I want each of you to observe the three objects and their interaction with the void. Then let's talk about what it means," Nadia instructed her team.

This observation coupled with the projection of the void coming in contact with their Home Orb left Nadia numb. She immediately got her father to pull together the top people he knew to review the team's work and finding's. She needed full confirmation of her and her team's modeling of the path of the black void and its intersection of their Orb before sharing it with anyone.

She wanted to shout for everyone to run and hide. It brought back memories of similar nightmares where she was trying to hide from the sun but could not find a hiding place. Even back in the tunnels the sun would find her.

It took another full three cycles for the review team to get together. Meanwhile Nadia reviewed all previous work.

"I have asked you to come here to review the data defining the discovery of a new phenomenon. The estimate of this phenomenon's attractive strength is unprecedented.

Our Orb and this phenomenon will very likely interact with each other within the next three cycles around our Central Orb," was Nadia's kickoff at the beginning of the meeting.

She was awed by the brain power in the room and thankful to Raulens for having called together the leading thought leaders in the field. It confirmed her suspicion on how important the matter was to him. These were people that were hard to get together so quickly.

Only Raulens could have pulled this meeting off. A few had already participated earlier with Raulens to verify the finding of the black void. Others had been pulled in because of their influence.

She then followed with the prepared presentation, brought out photos, provided each participant with the analysis package and data used to do the analysis. They all had access to any computing support they might request. She put her team at their disposal.

"I will now step back and let you decide how to proceed. My team needs your review and confirmation or repudiation. My team would be relieved if you found an error. We will be pleased to provide you with any additional data and information you request but I look to you to reach your own conclusions," Nadia stepped away from the center of the room.

Raulens took the lead as he and Nadia had discussed. He would ensure the proceedings focused on the correctness of the analysis performed by her team. He also wanted part of the team to review the calculation of the probable strength of the object.

Finally, he pointed out to a review of the path being modeled of the phenomenon and its interaction with the Grand Orb system.

Nadia pulled her team together and let them know that they were to relax and recover. They would wait until confirmation was given.

The meetings and analysis lasted for three work cycles. This was longer than expected. All in attendance cleared their schedule as they began to comprehend the seriousness of the issue.

Each step of the analysis confirmed Nadia's previous findings.

This caused heightened concern within the review group. They reworked every analysis but finally concluded there were no errors.

They confirmed the fact that the unknown phenomenon and their Orb would indeed come in contact with each other.

"The team has affirmed the work you have done. It is alarming and totally life altering. There is much that must be done in preparing for this potentially ultimate event. We each will be supporting your reports, conclusions, and suggestions," Raulens reported back at the closing of the evaluation meeting.

The meeting ended and some of the best minds on the Orb walked out with concerned looks and a few had tears in their eyes.

Raulens set about contacting all the influential leaders in government that he knew. Rapid action needed to occur, and he was going to ensure it would happen.

He knew their way of life was over. The third Orb that had been his focus suddenly fell off the cliff of more critical concern.

Survival for their species would mean fleeing their Orb or burrowing deeper than they had time for. With their current capability and the limited amount of time they could only be able to save a small portion of their population.

There was no recourse.

Raulens would rally all those he could and get them to take action. He would then demand that the leaders take the swift action needed to save the lives of as many beings as possible.

He was already repurposing the use of his rockets intended for the exploration of the third Orb to take as many of the Orbians off the orb in hopes of saving enough of them to reseed his kind somewhere in the Grand Orbian system.

Nadia contacted Keren and scheduled a review with him. She knew that he would be critical in quickly changing the political environment.

"Dad has already confirmed my findings. Our Orb and this unknown powerful void will come in close proximity within three cycles around the Grand Orb. I need your help in preparing our people for survival," Nadia said as she and her team began to take Keren through their findings.

Keren listened and asked clarification questions. He was convinced of the findings. It sent him reeling. All his expansion plans for the future were made void. He needed to refocus his efforts the on survival of the Orbians versus their expansion.

"I am walking away from this meeting as a changed person. All my ambitions and visions of the future have been altered. I will work with you and this team to implement whatever survival scenarios we can come up with. I feel a hollow void in my soul," Keren commented to Nadia at the end of the meeting.

Nadia looked around at her team and then responded that she and her team had already experienced the hollow feeling and did so each time they presented their materials. They were the messengers not of a bright future but individuals bearing a message of doom.

Little did either Keren or Nadia know the tremendous and unimaginable impact that they would each have in saving the Orbians.

Chapter 6: Lamins

$\mathcal{L}$amins Evington was the boy next door. He had grown up
with, played with, and was a true friend to both Keren and Nadia.
He was two orb cycles younger than Nadia. Lamins adored both
of his friends. He knew he more than adored Nadia. As they
grew up, he was their shadow. He was forever making sure that
he was with them whenever possible. He liked the fact that each
of the two always came up with something that was interesting
and challenging to do. He was also aware that both of his idols
liked him and included him on their adventures.

It was an understatement to say the Namens were an integral
part of the Evington family life. The Evintons and the Namens
were lifelong friends. His mother, Triansa, and Nadia's mother
were friends before either of them chose a mate.

"Aunt" Milan and his mother had grown up together in the
same warren. They were both farmers' daughters. They went to
their primary school together and later they attended Ulm
University and were roommates.

They both had focused on food. His mother had become a very successful Chef. Her best friend, Milan, became the supplier of new foods to utilize in the kitchen. They actually spent time together inventing new dishes. The two would create new dishes with the new plants and vegetables Milan developed.

Lamins was always their taste tester. This was the greatest reward they could bestow on him.

Milan and his mother dated and married almost at the same time. His father a lead engineer in an engines design and fabrication company could afford to move the family into a home next door to the Namens. His wife would have had it no other way. They moved into the same warren were they all still lived.

He knew that both of their families could afford to move to some of the new outer apartments with a great view of the canyon but had decided that they were happy in the homes they had.

From little on Lamins was fascinated and bewitched by Nadia. She was always friendly, but she never saw him as anything more than a warren friend.

On the other hand, as he grew, she became the measure of all the other girls and later young women he met. This worked to his disadvantage since none measured up to Nadia and he soon lost interest in them. His thoughts always returned to Nadia.

Keren was like the older brother Lamins never had. Lamins was the only cub in his family. Lamins looked up to Keren and got a lot of the how-to coaching from him. Keren later guided him in his social engagements. There was no one he could think of that had helped as much as Keren. Keren was the older brother he never had.

For Lamins there was no question about going on to Ulm University. His mother would have it no other way. He would have gone on his own. He needed no push. Nadia was his focus and that was where she was. He entered Ulm and in his second Orbian cycle he chose the field of Star Field Mapping and Investigation. It was a new field that interested him, and it put him in the same branch of the Ulm system, as Nadia. It also provided him the occasional excuse to run into her. He saw to it that his route and hers crossed as often as possible.

Lamins realized immediately he would need to excel if he were ever to measure up to Nadia's stellar expectations.

He watched as male after male made attempts for her attention. He was relieved when each was politely refused. He knew being a few cycles younger and her childhood friend made it even harder for him to compete for her attention.

Her polite refusals of the other competitors relieved Lamins.

"This at least gives me time to get better," Lamins thought to himself as he made a point of going to dinner at the same restaurant, he knew Nadia frequented.

He sought Keren's advice about his predicament. Lamins fixation on Nadia had been obvious to Keren for a long time. Keren had wisely stayed out of the middle of this situation. He advised an oblique approach.

"Join her group of friends and become familiar and be an integral member. Later work on the rest," Keren advised. He was not sure Lamins would ever break the Nadia shield, but he was not going to discourage the person that he considered like a younger brother.

Lamins took this advice and dated one of Nadia's friends. He slowly made his way into Nadia's close group. The group of friends didn't date each other so his entrance link to Nadia's friend was put aside in a friendly manner. He became active in the group and soon he was the main organizer for the group. In this way he was able to enjoy Nadia's company and to have her participate in the experiences he wanted them to have together. He was not alone with her, but he was with her. He remained quiet and did not push for anything more.

Keren watched from the side lines and said nothing. He knew better then to get in the middle of emotions guided by the heart. He had his own heart to deal with and that was all the confusion he needed. It seemed to him that Lamins was the right partner for Nadia but there was no way for him to intervene. He figured either nature would take its own course or the two of them might for ever stay only as friends.

At Ulm, Lamins worked his head off. He excelled in his field by sheer hard work and untold hours of study. Unlike Nadia, or Keren who seemed to absorb the knowledge like the rays descending on the Grand Orb, Lamins worked long and hard and made his way through by sheer determination to keep up with the two of them. He was usually exhausted by the end of each study and later each work cycle.

He took every course taught by "Uncle" Raulens and did special project work with his guidance. Raulens was even more imposing than Nadia, but Lamins did his best work in his classes. The insights and coaching he received from his "Uncle" provided the knowledge that put him at the head of his class.

He graduated number one in his class and landed a top offer at the new space complex. He eagerly went into his new job and was soon noticed for his breakthrough thinking and accomplishments.

The group of friends continued their association as they went into their various fields. This provided Lamins periodical association with Nadia. He looked forward to these moments when the "group" came together. As time went by the members of the group slowly found mates and lessened or stopped their participation.

He continued to plan the activities for the group. A core group always made the meetings, and the rest came when it fit into what they were doing with their families.

Lamins worked in the mapping and navigation group. He was tasked with mapping the location of all known objects and determining the path or route to travel to those locations designated as potential points of interest.

He built a computerized model that took in all the Grand Orbs satellites. He kept improving it, but he was not sure what its value might be.

This work was not of deep interest to him until the day the news of the confluence was announced. Then he began a detailed study the location of all the orbs in the Grand Orb system and all the objects surrounding the Orbs.

He developed his model into a series of three-dimensional space maps designating the optimum routes based on when the journey began, and which orb would be visited.

This he knew was breakthrough work.

The feature making Lamins' three-dimensional maps unique was their ability to adjust their information based on the complex movement of the objects in the Grand Orb system. These were dynamic maps showing the situation at the time the viewer was looking at them. They were projected in three dimensions in a darkened empty space in front of the observer. The observer could walk around the three-dimensional projection and be oriented from their position. The projected maps were constantly updating based on the feed of the orbiting telescopes.

The system also had a built in a zoom feature that supported the user when they wanted to get a closer look at the details of the region, they were interested in.

In different circumstances his work would have catapulted him up in the organization. However, his breakthrough came at the extraordinary moment of Nadia's doomsday discovery and the need for his models put him into an intense spotlight. It was not the spotlight he had sought but it was one that put him in constant contact with Nadia.

When he presented it to her, she gave him one of the few hugs she had ever given him. It sent his heart beating. She didn't know it, but she had given him the ultimate reward for the development of the mode.

Nadia became an ardent user of his mapping projection system and consulted with him on a constant basis. The two of them would spend hours together reviewing the path of the void and the movement of the Orbs in the Grand Orbian system.

"Are you confident in the mapping and movement calculations of your system," Nadia asked more than a few times.

She had run his model over and over to get an idea of the interaction of their Orb and the on-coming void. The result was always the same. There was a head on collision in the making.

He replied that he was constantly reviewing and adjusting the parameters of his model and its projections and unfortunately, he had found no significant error. The projection was accurate.

These were not ordinary times. His work was indeed noticed by a few key people, and it put him on an unexpected list.

The group of survivors needed to be selected and a list was indeed being drawn up.

Unknown to Lamins he was on that list and the person who and the reason why, he had been put on the list would have been a surprise to him as well.

Chapter 7: Namens Family Action

The family remained in the warren and the house where Nadia and Keren had grown up. The Namens never moved from their original home. Though they could easily afford to move, they were not attracted by the glamour of the homes in the more exclusive districts with views into the canyon. They were a humble family who enjoyed unprecedented fame. They were a very close family who together explored their Orb both physically and mentally. They were now together for their usual family gathering. The realization of the impending doom weighed heavily.

The mood was subdued.

Nadia looked around the table at her mother, father, and brother. Each was a major contributor to the good of their planet. Her heart was heavy. She felt she was the least of the four and now her discovery was one of impending doom.

"I feel so sad at having my great discovery be a doomsday event. All of you have done so much to improve the lives of those around us. I see no way for the way of life as we know it to survive the upcoming encounter with a region in space that ingests huge meteors. I have studied every scenario using Lamins newly developed three-dimensional mapping and visual projection system and it always comes to the same devastating result," Nadia said as she looked across at everyone.

She had tears in her eyes and could barely control her voice.

"You are not responsible for the Orb altering impact of your finding. We need to think how the people of our Orb might be able to survive this encounter.

Is there a way to blunt the interaction of the two?

Is there a way for us to survive in the mantel?

How will we activate our population to define the course of action to take?" Keren responded in his usual analytical mode.

He too was greatly disturbed by Nadia's discovery. His thinking was into counter actions and determining what could be done. He envisioned survival chambers that needed to be made in the mantel.

"This event will alter all our actions. What we have done up to this time is of little importance. How we behave and act in the near future will be a test of our ourselves and of our civilization.

Everyone has their hopes and dreams, but the Universe is without judgment or feeling. It is what it is, and we are who we are. I suggest we do our best. There will be no one to save us. We will need to take the best actions we can to save those we can.

We will try to ensure the survival of some fragment of our population. Defining who those survivors are to be, will be what tests our society and civilization," Milan spoke quietly.

What crossed her mind was not the end of civilization but the fact that her children would not have the pleasure of having and raising their own children. This thought broke her heart. Her tears were for their missed future.

"We need a way to escape our Orb or a way to alter its path so we will not encounter this catastrophe," Nadia spoke up.

She had spent countless hours trying to figure out a way to change the situation and had decided what must happen was for them to figure out how to survive the situation.

"My team has already done a quick analysis showing we will only be able to save about four thousand Orbians if we begin now to build spaceships and rockets. The initial evaluation of the interaction shows our Home Orb will be devastated.

Nadia said that she and her team had to continue to model the interaction and determine the forces the home Orb would experience.

She clarified that her initial review and understanding of the interaction that nothing would on the surface would survive.

The Orb' atmosphere and the oceans would be stripped from surface.

Nadia put her hands over her face and said that she could not speak any more about the horror she saw ahead for them.

Raulens wanted to speak of hope and what could be, but he also knew in this case there was no magic trick he could pull off to save them from doomsday ahead. There might be ways to save more Orbians by going into the mantel but that would still be a very limited number.

"We have only about three Major Orbital cycles before the encounter. We will need each other's support. We will all be in a state of shock, sometimes disbelief, sometimes very angry. We will not be in control of anything around us. We will have each other, and we must help each other," Raulens said in a somber tone as he walked around the table and gave each of them a hug and kiss.

The happiness he felt each day as he thought about the success of his immediate family was now replaced with a sadness he could not overcome.

"We will plan our family get together more often. We may need to do a lifetime of living in the next three cycles. I know we will do our best at trying to save our Orb, but it may well be beyond our control," Raulens continued.

"So, let's schedule the activities we want to do as a family. I want to hike the top of the canyon and name the constellations." Nadia spoke up.

She just wanted to hug all of them and hang onto them for as long as she could.

Milan invited their long-time neighbors and close friends, the Evintons, to join the Namens family at the top of the canyon and there together under the stars the two families shared their dinner.

They began dinner by explaining the situation to the Evintons. This was not new to them because Lamins had shared almost the same information previously. His special three-dimensional modeling capability had been the critical element that allowed for this early warning of their doomsday.

Then the discussion and focus turned to the stars in the heavens. Raulens, Nadia and Lamins shared their favorite objects in the sky and the stories that went them. The Evintons had some of their own stories that they shared.

Then they all walked to a point that overlooked the canyon and gazed at the works tending the fields illuminated by the powerful night lamps.

Lamins finally got to have the dinner under the stars he had wanted to have with Nadia. It was not the romantic dinner he had envisioned but none the less it was with the person he had always wanted to be with. He gave his thanks for this one bright spot in an otherwise sad and disturbing situation.

The two families agreed to gather together every ten work cycles for similar outings. They were indeed going to experience their lifetime of gatherings in the short time they had left, and they were going to do it as one family.

For Lamins this provided him experiences with the soul mate he had hoped to live a lifetime with. He did not try to push their relationship any farther. He decided he would be content to be close and feel her presence and be satisfied with what could be experience.

He had not counted on a short lifetime but planned to garnish it with the light of his life. He planned to seek the advice of his longtime "big brother," and mentor to see if there was anything else he could do.

Chapter 8: Survival Actions

Keren set up a series of meetings in the Council. At these meetings Nadia and Raulens presented their findings. Afterwards Keren and his most ardent political opponent jointly sponsored a survival committee that together they jointly were to lead.

Keren had foreseen the upcoming debates and potential delays. He had approached his strongest opponent and had shared the situation privately. It was amazing how much the two agreed on in this life and death situation. They both recognized that any delay would directly affect the survival of their people. Their cooperation galvanized the council and committed them to action.

The committee proved to be as problematic as expected. There were long debates as to how those to be saved would be selected. In the end science, age, and a desire to save a cross section of their heritage were the guidelines. Those to be saved would be young. They would genetically represent the entire race. A few older individuals would be selected based on the need to staff and to lead the small flotilla of spaceships.

The destination for these ships was discussed but the final destination selection was left to the scientists. There were not too many options and certainly no clear one from which to choose.

The selection design for those going up in the rockets was to create a lottery system populated with all individuals meeting a specific set of criteria. Individuals with the right profiles were selected and put into the survival population database. These individuals, if selected and their families would determine if they would accept a place to go out into space. If they accepted, they were then to be examined for health and mental factors. Once they passed this screening, they would be given special training to prepare them for their journey into space.

There were many who could not believe and would not accept such a dire fate awaited their Orb. They demanded and got additional reviews of the finding. They wanted their own scientists to review the analysis and the model of the interaction. An agreement to support this action was reached. The survival preparation and selection work would go ahead as the review took place. There would be no delay. It was clear that every moment was now precious.

The remaining time was short and the preparation for survival monumental. Financing the effort was discussed but Keren made and won the point that all resources regardless of cost should be focused on enhancing the survival potential of their race. If they survived, they would figure out how to straighten out the finances.

All the resources of Orb would go into the survival effort. Every needed resource would be made available with no thought given to cost.

The only critical item was the development and the execution of a master survival plan.

This monetary free approach greatly simplified and accelerated the ability of each critical team to take immediate action. "Execute the Survival Plan" became the phrase of the day. People flocked to volunteer centers to get their work reoriented to match the needs of the survival plan.

The government declared a state of emergency and put together a team to manage the preparation for the upcoming doomsday.

Rockets would be built, analysis of the situation would continue, those to be saved would be selected and trained.

Ideas to save those remaining behind were identified. Several projects, including establishing survival cells in the mantel tunnels were immediately commissioned.

Milan decided to build a self-contained survival area. She discussed this with Raulens, and they used their own funds to outfit the area. Keren provided an area recently excavated in the mantel expansion project. There Milan set up an aqua culture with plants and a legume farm growing in artificial light. She recruited friends to help.

Triansa became the manager of the area.

Krinsar was the main construction supervisor.

The two could operate without stirring up any specific interest in what was being done. This effort was kept quiet but progressed rapidly.

Housing along with the necessary sanitary support systems were planned and built. An oxygen generation system and an extensive recycling system were also set up.

Milan thought the odds of anyone surviving for long after the confluence with the anomaly in space was minimal but she none the less put all her energy and resources into the effort. There were really few other actions for her to take. Her experiences with her own project proved to be prophetic when Nadia asked her to help outfit the rockets going to space in the same way as she was outfitting the survival chamber.

She immediately understood Nadia's vision.

Nadia wanted the spaceships to have their own gardens as a means to grow food and enough plants to rejuvenate and generate the oxygen needed.

Raulens meanwhile gathered his team together and reviewed the situation. The team looked to him for guidance. After the shock wore off, they were eager to make a difference.

"We developed our rockets with the hope of exploring the third orb. Now we must build enough of these rockets to save as many of our race as possible. I estimate we will be able to build about twenty rockets and be able to outfit them with enough fuel, and food to make the journey to the third orb. Technically, we are capable of making such a journey. However, the radiation is still the major obstacle to this journey. We must look at ways to improve the shielding." Raulens shared at one of the early planning meetings.

He felt that with enough water shielding a habitable space going environment could be created.

"We might as well send up as much water as possible. What we have on the orb will most likely be lost," Raulens pointed out to his team.

His team took up the challenge to design and build as many vessels as possible. A multi-hulled design was quickly agreed on. The outside skin would be a one-half inch ceramic layer lined with lead and gold. This ceramic layer would provide the needed structural strength and about five percent of the shielding. The next layer would be two inches of densely packed soil followed by another one-half inch ceramic layer lined with lead and gold. Then a chamber six inches across would be filled with water. The inside would be another one-half inch thick ceramic layer lined with lead and gold. This would provide insulation, radiation shielding, and the structural strength that far exceeded anything they had come up with before.

This design was reviewed and once the propulsion team agreed they would have the boost power to launch the rocket, the building began immediately.

The newly built rocket center near Ulm was expanded. There would be ten missile tubes in all. An additional ten rockets would be launched from the surface. These pads consisted of pouring three solid leg stands to hold the weight of the rockets. The soil around the stands was highly compacted to provide resistance to the rocket blast. This was a fast and adequate design for a single use launch pad. It also allowed for a rocket size variation.

The ten rockets to be built in the silos would be larger in size and diameter then the ten rockets to be launched from the surface. The ten surface rockets would be built in the other cities and their diameter was limited by the diameter able to be transported through the tunnel system. These rockets had to come up the elevators in sections and then be assembled on the surface.

The number of workers at the center increased tenfold. What had been considered a spacious design now seemed cramped.

The laboratories were all extremely busy. Breakthroughs in electronics and communication occurred almost on a daily basis.

The amount of construction material flowing into each of the launch tubes created a logistical jam at all the elevator points.

The launch and escape plans were developed and reviewed. Nadia and her team proposed two escape and survival scenarios.

The first was a fast, direct dash to the third planet.

The second went in the opposite direction. This second scenario was a journey outward in the solar system in search for an alternate home.

She came up with these two because of her discussions with Raulens' team and with scientists and doctors who predicted as high as a fifty per cent fatality rate in trying to reach the third orb. Then there was the additional challenge of surviving on the third orb itself. The gravity of the orb would be the final test of their will to survive. This gravity might kill the few survivors to make it that far.

The first choice remained the third orb. Nadia had doubts about the dual challenges of overcoming the radiation and the greatly increased pull of gravity. She kept that doubt to herself because she had almost the same doubts about survival on the path outward. She, however, was determined to develop the outward journey as a viable alternative.

She insisted on an alternate rocket ship design plan that would allow the rockets to be used to establish a system that would generate enough force to simulate Orbian gravity. Such a ship would travel outward through the solar system and try alternate locations on satellites around the giant outer Orbs.

This was debated but Nadia would not let this choice die.

She was unstoppable in her demand for alternatives.

Raulens met his match in the discussion about this second alternative. He realized Nadia was determined to have this alternative build into the design of the rockets. He challenged his design team to come up with a design that would achieve what Nadia was demanding. The team responded and drew up a design that could be assembled in space.

Nadia and her team took up the challenge to examine the third orb in detail and also to determine where it would be when they encountered the black void.

The third Orb would be almost on the opposite side of the Grand Orb from her Home Orb. This meant they would need to spend an extensive length of time in a high radiation area. She wished her Home Orb would have been on that far side. If it had been then she and the population on her Orb would not be under this tremendous stress at trying to figure out how to survive. The third Orb was far enough away that it would not face the same danger even if it had been on this side.

Nadia enrolled and organized all the other astronomers on the planet to study each of the outer Orbs and the satellites circling around them. The focus was to find a location where a survival colony could be established. There was no problem in getting the resources enrolled and eagerly studying these Orb systems.

Everyone on the Orb was now focused on creating the situation for the survival of their species.

Within one Orb cycle, Nadia became the face, the voice, and the survival strategist everyone began to look to for direction.

The family recognized this immediately.

Nadia was doing this without thinking. She was passionate and articulate about ensuring the survival of her species. She encouraged alternatives but examined each option in such detail she was constantly challenging every team involved in the effort. She challenged them to make improvements and to think beyond their current limitations. She insisted that it was time to think beyond the normal and think about the impossible and then make it happen.

She was the youngest of all the leaders around her, but they all looked to her for guidance and inspiration. Her songs about hope and survival were constantly on the air.

She became the heart, the soul, and the brains of the survival movement.

Raulens became her constant coach and advisor. He recognized her as having a powerful mind that was pouring every ounce of her being into making survival a reality. His efforts focused on supporting Nadia to make sure she did not break down before it was time to launch.

He also realized she would need to be one of the people going out with the rockets. No one else would have the breadth of knowledge or the drive for survival and the influence needed to ensure those on the rockets would act to ensure survival. He privately discussed this with Keren and with other members on the Survival Selection Committee.

The average age of the planet's population was seventeen cycles. The normal life expectancy was thirty-five cycles. Seven was the median age selected for the survivors.

This age was determined to give the survivors sufficient years to establish colonies and still have time to reproduce. The entire survival group would represent a mix of gender, age, and DNA.

Keren was co-leader of the Survivor Selection Board. There were only a few appointed positions in the survival group. These appointed positions were, a Captain for each ship, two Navigators, one astronomer and one overall Mission Leader.

He ensured Nadia was selected to go as the astronomer and also be the overall mission leader. Once nominated by Keren and discussed by the board, her selection was unopposed. All recognized her as a key leader in the survival effort and the right person to guide the survivors in establishing colonies. There were a few questions about family connection, but these were quickly dispelled. There was no other person so well suited to lead the survivors.

Never one to be locked into one course of action, Nadia also pushed her team to look for all other locations where a colony could be established. All eight planets and their moons were evaluated. Each potential location received a more in-depth evaluation. Few additional sites were found.

Two moons on the sixth orb out were promising. There was one moon circling the seventh orb. A few more promising moons were on the eighth orb, but the current observation capabilities prevented them from verifying their efficacy. This verification would be done if and when these moons became objects of interest.

Nadia took a tour of the aqua and indoor gardens Milan had developed.

She immediately enrolled Milan in designing and supervising the construction of gardens for every rocket. This fit with Nadia's vision of a long-term journey outward. If this were required the survivors would need a way to grow their own food, to generate their own air and to create the materials to build with.

When asked about this, Nadia's response was simple, "What if these survivors end up spending more time in space than planned? Will we send them out only to starve in space?"

No more questions were asked. Milan ensured each rocket got a garden designed into its structure.

Nadia next approached Raulens and inquired about the progress being made in establishing gravitation on the rockets.

"Well, the only way to simulate gravity would be to configure the vessels into a rotating wheel. If the survivors need to spend a great deal of time in space the equivalent force of gravity would ensure their health. I will draw up a way the rockets we send up can be arranged to form such a vessel should it be needed," Raulens shared with Nadia.

He was impressed with his daughter's comprehensive identification and development of the possible options.

Keren informed Raulens and Milan of Nadia's selection as the Astronomer and Mission leader for the survivor group.

Nadia was to be informed soon but until it became public, the family members were to keep quiet. They knew it would weigh heavy on Nadia to be selected when her family would be left behind.

The knowledge gave a boost to Raulens and Milan. They wished Keren would be going as well but his work in the guiding of the government would prohibit it.

Those selected would all face a feeling of relief and guilt. Family members would feel both happiness and remorse. The finality of this situation left no one untouched or at ease.

Keren and his team decided notification would wait until formal training had to begin.

They had only a three cycle time periods to accomplish the impossible.

It was not enough time. They all knew it was not enough time, but it was the oncoming black void that had established the time frame.

Every corner was cut, and every activity was expedited. The materials needed to finish the rocket interiors were packed into the rockets. The crew of survivors would be tasked with finishing the work.

It was critical to get each rocket ready to launch. And it was critical to develop enough capability in a very young crew. Training would begin one half Orb cycle before the encounter. This was the shortest time span possible and would allow for the final confirmation of the actual doomsday scenario.

Nadia was in the middle of the whirl wind. Not only did she continue to work with her astronomy team, but she became very active in determining what would go up in the rockets with the survivors. She enrolled a cross section of specialists from farmers, scientists, and city planners. She chartered this team to determine what should be in the rockets to ensure long term survival.

She established a survival training course for those individuals that were on the selection list. The number to be selected slowly increased with the completion of each additional rocket. She wanted those in the rockets to be able to support themselves for multiple lifetimes.

During all this time Nadia survived on a minimum of sleep. She lost fifteen percent of her body weight.

Lamins made it a point to share a daily meal with her. He caught her wherever she would be and made her eat enough for her to survive. He had enrolled several of their friends to make sure Nadia did not forget to take care of herself.

"She will kill herself with the intensity that she is using herself," Lamins shared with Keren.

"I think you should make sure she has you to lean on and you should make sure she makes it through," Keren had replied.

Keren was working one other item that would affect Nadia, but he kept that to himself.

The day to announce the survivor group members arrived. Private messages were sent out to all those selected or their family head. In most cases the selected survivors were minors, and their parents would determine if they would remain on the list.

Nadia got the message of her selection. She took her selection as hard as her family had expected. She did not feel deserving. She announced that she could not accept leaving them behind.

Keren helped her accept the situation when he pointed out she would be the oldest of those selected and one of the most critical members in ensuring the survival of their race.

He highlighted her ability to identify the need for the gardens, the oxygen generators, a recycle system and the creation of gravity to ensure the health of the survivors.

"We feel if anyone can ensure success, it is you," Keren said with true sincerity. We have placed you as Mission Commander and Astronomer. Originally this was to be two separate positions. Your selection allowed one more individual to be selected.

After accepting the situation, Nadia immediately brought the leadership team together. She quickly realized she indeed was the most knowledgeable about the options for survival. There were twenty captains ranging from eleven to fourteen Orb cycles in age.

At sixteen, Nadia was the oldest.

She was surprised to find out that Lamins was to be second in command. He was almost fifteen.

The mission navigator was fifteen and the second navigator was fourteen.

Nadia looked down the list of the leaders of the survival group. The group was young and inexperienced. By design the genders were equal. The remaining survival group members were all several years younger. The age was from four to eight cycles.

Each rocket would lift off with two hundred survivors.

She kept thinking about the numbers. Only four thousand out of more than one billion people would make this final journey.

Tears were in Nadia's eyes as she put the document with all the names back on her desk. She continued to put away her belongings and pack what she would take on the rocket. Her most treasured item was a picture of her family taken on one of their recent outings.

"This is just not real," she kept thinking to herself as she dried her tears.

Nadia had been instrumental in deciding on the content of the rockets. She took the time to review all the selected items. She especially focused on the gardens and recycle centers.

"We have used all the lead and gold on the planet. Family heirlooms have been sacrificed. All the lead available has been gathered. These rockets have the best shielding possible. The radiation going in toward the third orb might still prove to be too formidable," Raulens warned as the two walked away from their garden inspection tour.

"Yes, that is why I have insisted on the second plan and a system that can generate gravity," Nadia replied.

Her studies of the solar system had identified a few potential sites on moons around the outer planets. The prospects were barely sufficient and would never have been of interest if it were not for the upcoming catastrophe.

She outfitted the rockets with the materials to sustain the journey outward. The gardens Milan designed and built were critical for the survival of those who would leave the planet. Nadia identified the garden care takers and had Milan train them and her leadership team. She wanted each rocket was set up and organized to be self-sufficient.

Raulens designed the rockets to be assembled in two different configurations.

The most radiation shielding configuration was for the rockets to cluster around a central rocket. This would provide the maximum radiation shielding in the center.

The second configuration was to create a rotating wheel. This second way provided a rotational force simulating their Home Orb gravity. It, however, would provide the least shielding.

Since this work would be done out in space, Nadia had Raulens review the design and instruct the leadership team on how to create each of the two arrangements. Nadia insisted that this be done until each leader could verbally recite the instructions. Nadia was adamant about the leadership knowing how to manage the rockets in space. There would be no room for error.

"Nadia has become the epitome of her father," Keren commented to Lamins as the two examined the exoskeletons being modified to go on the rockets.

It would be the job of the survival crew to actually do the physical work of assembling either structure. There was also the work of finishing the interior of each rocket. There were only 1000 space suits for the four thousand survivors. The matching exoskeletons would provide additional strength to each of the thousand.

Nadia hoped the number of suits would be sufficient. On the other hand, she wondered if there would be enough individuals capable to use the suits effectively.

She was prepared to be one of the users of the exoskeletons and spacesuits.

She had Keren train her in the use of exoskeletons until she could pick up a class of water and bring it to her mouth and allow her to drink it.

Keren told her that she was the first and only person who had mastered the exoskeleton to that degree.

Little did either know that her skill, determination, and personal drive would result in the survival of their race far into the future.

Chapter 9: Launch Preparation

To Nadia the confluence of the void with the Grand Orb system appeared to be a synchronized journey. The Grand Orb system slowly approached the void and the void seemed to travel directly toward the fourth Orb.

Lamins pointed out that in actuality only the Grand Orb system was moving. He pointed out that the black void was stationary. Once took that into account the modeling became more exact and clearly confirmed that their Orb would pass very close to the void.

Lamins was in charge of this modeling effort. His understanding of the three-dimensional movements of the Grand Orb system and the space surrounding it made him the obvious choice to lead this effort. He and the astronomers observing the void verified and sharpened Nadia's initial calculations.

The Home Orb and the void would indeed intersect.

There was no longer any doubt or debate. Even the most extreme opponents were silenced.

A desperate haste now descended on survival preparation. Every resource was being poured into the building of rockets to be used to save as many Orbians possible.

There were a variety of other survival projects, but they would only save a very small number of additional Orbians.

One such project was being quietly led by Milan. She was leading an effort to establish a survivor's colony deep in the mantle just outside of the city of Ulm. The location was a large area that Keren had excavated. The plan was to survive the confluence and then re-establish the population afterwards. This colony would only hold one thousand people. She lamented the fact that it was such a small part of the population, but it was all she could accomplish. This was a survival group she, Raulens, Keren, Triansa, Krinsar and a few other leaders personally funded and established. Similar groups around the globe had formed to try and save portions of the population.

The majority of the population continued to function very much as always. Less long-term work got done but the cycle-to-cycle activities continued.

More families went on various simple outings together. This was a society of family and lifelong family bonds.

There seemed to be a rise of civility. The intensity of living was reduced to a cycle-to-cycle activity and action.

"We are after all showing our best side," Milan shared with her family.

"Yes, we are rising to show our best side," Nadia agreed.

The only significant difference was the fact that many families moved closer together. Those working far from family came home. Even those, only living a little more than walking distance away, moved closer together.

The selection of those to be sent up on the rockets in hopes that the Orbian race could be reseeded began in earnest.

Those with family members selected for survival, moved to Ulm.

Fifty percent of the survival crew was between the ages of four and eight cycles in age. They were specifically selected young in anticipation that they would need to survive for a great period of time before they could re-establish a colony.

These members met daily and participated in a variety of training, instruction, and conditioning.

Nadia made a point of meeting every survivor member and their family. She shared with them what their role on the survival crew would be.

She spent extra time with the families with the younger cubs. These younger members were teamed up with and introduced to an older member. Nadia arranged for the older survivor member to meet daily and spend a few hours together with the younger survivor member and their family.

She knew this early association would make it easier for the younger member as well as the family when it came time to part. The families of the teamed members spent time together. This allowed a closer bonding to occur. Those from the other canyons were staying in apartments and dorms around the University of Ulm.

Each day the families would accompany and watch the survival training that was taking place. This training focused on movement in a no gravity situation. This was carried out in water pools where the act of being weightless could be simulated. It was rigorous and tough and many of those being trained were stressed to their limits.

Nadia made sure that each of them had both parents and others there to give encouragement and comfort.

Those that would go out into space practiced getting into their space suits and then getting into the pool to assemble and connect various objects. These practices lasted an entire work cycle. There were at least three separate practices per cycle.

Nadia drove herself to watch and coach as many of these groups as possible.

"Each of you tasked with the responsibility of going out into space to assemble and setup our designated structure will be able to do so with your eyes closed," Nadia said as she addressed the crew she was coaching.

"There is no room for error. There is no forgiveness of a mistake," She continued. "Everyone must look out for themselves, and everyone will have a partner that you must look after as well," she added.

She had a suit and exoskeleton for her use. She practiced with every group and individual until she too could do any task with her eyes closed.

Her actions seemed to motivate those she was coaching.

She was making sure that those who went into space would have the survival skills that they would need.

They were young but they were being asked to do more than most Orbian adults.

The rockets were scheduled to be put into orbit thirty Orbian cycles prior to the confluence. "Confluence" had become the word describing the upcoming catastrophe. It was a meeting no one wanted but it seemed inevitable. The distance and time to this "Confluence" was shown on every communication channel as a doomsday countdown clock.

The departure of the rockets from the planet would occur only if required. There was still hope the planet could withstand the meeting with the void. The scientific community continued to debate the extent of the damage the Orb would experience. All supported the effort and actions being taken but some could not concede the Orb would be destroyed or unable to support life afterwards.

Raulens and his followers knew there would be little left of the Orb after the meeting.

His focus was in preparing for the launch of the rockets. He drove himself as hard as he saw his daughter doing.

Milan's focus was the preparation of the survival chamber.

Raulens' main contribution to the survival chamber effort was in the design of the massive doors to close off the chamber. He pushed the design to be ten times stronger than originally planned. He got some resistance but insisted on his design and drove the construction to meet his specification and design.

On the cycle before the launch, Nadia spent more time with her family.

Raulens, Milan and Keren had all come to terms with their fate. The Evintons were also at peace. Both families would fight to the end. Milan and Triansa had the deep in mantle survivor's enclave completed. The site had been built, outfitted and the one thousand participants had been moved in.

The site existence and location were a public secret. Everyone was concerned that at the last moment there might be a panic rush to escape death. Raulens and Milan came to the conclusion their time in the survival enclave would be short if the devastation were at the level predicted by Lamins' modeling. They had oxygen generators but in the long term they needed a supply of oxygen from the planet. They shared none of their concern with Nadia.

The two families went together on Nadia's favorite walk along the canyon top. They viewed the orbital system through the observatory telescope.

At sunrise, the families and Nadia's longtime friends took the tram across the valley and walked along the latest gardens developed by Milan.

Nadia's closest friends put their defiant hands together in the sunlight one more time. They all gave a cheer for Nadia.

This time Lamins was with her. He had his hand on hers as the group raise their hands one last time, in defiance.

Then they all returned to the family home to share dinner. This was a menu made up of the various favorites each had identified.

Conversation was light and focused on good memories. Each knew the launch to occur would be final.

Nadia and Lamins were the only members going up to space.

They and their friends and families would never be together again. This was a devastating feeling in a culture where family was one's main identity.

Chapter 10: Launch, Wait, Escape

The millions of stars overhead glimmered and twinkled. Anyone walking and looking up would marvel at the beauty to be seen in the sky. What could not be seen was the black void that the planet would soon meet. They could not see doom but there was little doubt that is was going to visit their beloved Orb.

The beings of the planet had never faced such a threat. Their planet had almost been destroyed and yet they had survived and risen. There was hope they would do it again but this time they were going to meet with an unknown force beyond what they could imagine.

Nadia and her team had done their job. They felt miserable about having been the messengers of doom. Nadia found it hard not personalize and not assume that it was her fault.

Now only a few Grand Orb cycles later she stood with her space leadership team in front of the four thousand survivor group members. The entire survivor contingent was surrounded by their parents and close family members. The only other people present were the launch support ground crew and the a few news media personnel. All together there were at least twenty-five thousand people in the launch area.

Nadia was aware of the silence as she approached the speakers stand. She looked slowly around and took a moment to let the situation sink into her mind. She had thought a great deal about this moment and of what to say. It was a moment that would be a farewell that had never before been voiced. It was a farewell that would live with each of the survivors for their entire life and a farewell that was being sent to a billion for one last time.

She slowly and softly said, "I am humbled to be a part of and to lead this survival group. I have spent my time with each survival member, and I know they have feelings similar to mine. We are humbled; we are saddened, we feel grief, our hearts ache.

This will, we know, be an ache that we will carry throughout our life cycle. There is an aching pain in our hearts for our friends, for our families and all whose lives we leave at risk here on our Home Orb.

There is also a great chasm of fear and concern that we will not be adequate in our endeavors.

We are called the survivor group. Survival is your wish and dream and you have generously given it to us. However, I am aware of the many perils ahead and the tough choices we survivors may need to make. I promise to guide this group, to keep it safe and to ensure we indeed survive.

Together we will do our best. If necessary, we will travel the entire solar system in our survival journey. Let me assure you our history, our culture, our memories, our families will not be forgotten. We as a species are at risk of annihilation but we will not go silently into oblivion. We will fight, we will create, and we will leave our mark on this Grand Orb system. The future will find either our success and our species still in existence, or a clear history of our valiant effort at survival. We will leave our Orbian footprint on this orbital system. We will leave our mark. We will be your footprints in the sands of time.

To each family on this Orb, may these remaining days be ones of togetherness and harmony." Nadia ended with the traditional Orbian saying.

She stood silently for a minute and turned to leave the speakers stand. The traditional recognition of chit, chit, chit rose to a roar as the audience recognized her and the entire survivor group.

The survivor members each followed their captains toward their respective rockets. Nadia had taken the survivor group through this exit several times. She knew this would be the hardest time for all the members and family.

Each rocket had a representative age mix. The parents of the younger children sat with them and now relinquished them to the designated survivor partner.

Nadia had been right. The parting was very difficult but, because they knew the young person to whom they were passing their children, most hand offs, though tearful and emotional, went smoothly. There were only a couple of situations where a family member needed to be restrained and held back.

Nadia's rocket was to be the first to be launched. Each subsequent rocket would follow in a designated order. The launch had been set up as a continuous sequence of launches. The trigger for the next launch was the previous rocket successfully achieving its orbital height. As each crew got on board, the people on the plain were escorted to the tunnel entrance and off the launch area.

The ground crew made last minute checks on the rockets and launch control. The launch was directed from the space center control room. Each rocket had its own launch team. The launches followed a predetermined order.

The rockets in the launch tubes would be first. The ten rockets on the surface would be last. Each team waited for the call to launch. This call would come from the central monitoring command. Raulens, Milan and Keren watched the launches from Raulens' office next to the control room.

The launches began and continued throughout the night. Each captain acknowledged achieving orbit. Their next duty was to move the ship into a synchronized orbit with the Home Orb between the rocket and the Grand Orb.

Nadia began immediately to bring the rockets together to form a large rocket cluster. This would be the configuration to travel to the third Orb. The outer rockets would be filled with supplies and living quarters would be opened up in the inner rockets.

When the twentieth rocket launched, Raulens contacted Nadia.

"I am overjoyed all twenty rockets reached orbit safely. In normal times this would have been done over twenty orb cycles. I am pleased to have been able to see so many get launched. There will be one more rocket. It will not have anyone on board and will be launched and put into orbit in the next few cycles. It will have everything we have developed and some additional fuel and water. It will be filled with a variety of spare parts, equipment, and materials. This rocket did not get completely finished but it is able to launch. I am sure you will find it and the materials a useful addition to your efforts," Raulens messaged.

The ground crew quickly dismantled each launch station and moved the pre-identified materials into the final rocket. Nothing would go to waste.

The electronic communication equipment alone would make the launch useful. Equipment from laboratories, special materials, and anything Raulens believed would be useful was packet into the last rocket. He was sending everything of value he could think of out to Nadia.

"Thank you" was Nadia's simple reply.

She knew Raulens would have thought about and planned for almost every contingency. She wondered what she would find in the last rocket.

Nadia was immediately faced with her first obstacle. She and almost the entire crew was experiencing the nausea of weightlessness and the lack of gravity. This was one thing that had not been practiced or experienced by any of the crew.

She found it extremely hard to concentrate on her mission. She was tired and hungry but could not keep food down. Their practice session on the Orb was very valuable at experiencing weightlessness in the pool but it had not prepared them for the side effect that continuous weightlessness was now causing. Now, with her entire crew affected by this nausea she had to drive them to get all the rockets connected.

Nadia called her captains together and pushed them to keep the work on schedule. The many days of practice on the ground paid off. Her discipline and push kept the operation on track.

"I know how tough this is. Make it happen. Do what we practiced. We cannot, we will not fail on our first step," Nadia gave her encouragement.

The captains did a perfect job of positioning each rocket. They overcame their nausea and were excellent at coaching their teams. The joint pins came through the joining holes and were immediately bolted and the connection sealed.

The outer positioning ring sections were taken out by a crew of twenty space suited crew members. This was the most dangerous work the crew would undertake. The ring would strap all the rockets together. This arrangement locked and stabilized the entire rocket group.

Each person going out was tethered to the rocket. This proved to be critical. Several of the team actually floated away from the ship when they failed to realize their action would have an opposite response. Their practice on the ground quickly made the difference and the buddy system worked as it had been intended to work.

Meanwhile those staying inside moved their quarters toward the center and the variety of materials to the outward rockets. The goal was to provide additional radiation protection.

Though the rockets were being shielded by the Home Orb, the current radiation exposure was significantly higher than on the ground. Clustering the rockets reduced the radiation to an acceptable level. They would be exposed to an even higher radiation level on their inward journey toward the third Orb.

Nadia was becoming less sure of the journey inward toward the Grand Orb and the third orb.

Raulens had concluded the third planet was shielded from the greatly increased radiation by a magnetic field. This was the only way he could make sense of the abundant signs of life he had found. His measures of the effect of his own planet's magnetic protection verified those regions where the weak and distorted magnetic field was the strongest was where the radiation was the weakest.

Nadia was aware of this and hoped her cluster of ships could get inside of the magnetic shield of the third Orb.

Her primary goal was the third Orb, but she was not going to be caught off guard should their first goal become impossible. She and the captains spent time reviewing the work needed if they were to create an operating spaceship with centrifugal force acting as gravity. This was done each work cycle as they awaited the Confluence.

During this unreal, timeless wait Nadia had the crew completing the remaining inside work. The configuration for the inside was very dependent on how each rocket section was to be used. The least amount of work was for a fast transit to the third Orb. This was the work being done during the wait for the meeting with the black void.

The Grand Orb system was passing by the void but to those on the Home Orb and in the rockets, it appeared the void was bearing directly down on them.

The launch of the rockets had been made at what was thought to be the last possible moment. Even so it seemed like an eternity as they awaited the Confluence.

At the last possible moment, when the fate of the Home Orb was certain, Nadia gave the command for the rockets to leave their protected position.

"We four thousand are the hope or our doomed civilization, we are running for our future, but we will not forget out past," Nadia sent down her message and then she commanded her captains to fire their engines.

Nadia had her rockets begin their run for the third Orb as they watched the impending meeting.

It was a sight that would live in all of their memories for their entire lifecycle. The meeting of the void and Home Orb was a cataclysmal meeting.

As the Orb approached the void, she watched as the atmosphere was pulled away from the planet like the skin being peeled from a fish. It was actually visible as a thin layer of twisting and wavering white mist as it made the transit across the black of space toward the black void.

The telescope in Nadia's orbital observatory showed the event in painfully clear detail. This telescope was linked to the computer system and was broadcast throughout the ships. Nadia wanted to make sure every member of the crew saw the fate of their Home Orb.

It was a moment that should be permanently imprinted in each of their souls.

They all watched as the waters of the seas followed in an upward swirling straw-like path. A constant plume of air, water and all materials on the surface was lifted as if it was being vacuumed from a rug. It was as if the soul was leaving the Orb's body and traveling out to the black mouth of the void. Even as a constant stream of air, water and much of the top layer of the Orb was pulled away by the void, the rotation of the Orb seemed to be challenging the void, but the pull of the void caused a gigantic wall of water to travel around the Orb and through the deep canyons.

The rotation of the orb created a twenty click high wall of water that traveled at a speed equal to the rotation speed of the Orb but back toward the side of the void. The tremendous forces of the wall of water scrubbed the surface clean of all structures. The walls at the top of the canyons were pulled up and out toward the void. The sound wave traveling out before the massive wall of water gave those ahead a few moments notice of their impending death.

The winds picked up speed as it was pushed ahead of the water. At first the wind reminded those standing out before it of spring and hope. But swiftly, the winds howled and sang the cold song of death.

The millions standing bravely and facing the impending doom were instantly pulverized by the un-measurable forces of the wall of water that ripped the life from the surface of the Orb. Finally, the water lifted outward towards the void, and all was pulled through space.

The air had appeared as a ghost, the water was a blue stream mixed with every imaginable object on the Orb. It was a solid stream of green, grey, black, and blue swirling and reflecting the light in a ballroom glitter ball fashion. The horrible difference was that the light reflections that were cast were the reflections of death.

The occupants on the rockets watched in spell binding horror as the Home Orb's atmosphere, water and all life were peeled from the surface.

If space had allowed the occupants on the rockets would have heard the continuous groans and screams of the Home Orb's pain. They would have felt the searing pain of skin being ripped from the flesh. They would have tasted the acid bile of death.

As it was, they antiseptically witnessed the void swallowing the face, the skin, and the soul of their Orb. They knew their parents, brothers, sisters, lovers, and friends were all gone. The watchers would forever hear the silent screams and would feel their skin being ripped from their bodies.

They would forever try to grasp the enormity of the catastrophe they witnessed. The sight of the barren rock left behind could never be scrubbed from their souls. The eternal silent scream of the dying Orb was cast into the surrounding vacuum of space.

The mass of their Home Orb and its velocity carried it past the grasp of the void. It staggered on in its journey around the Central Orb. It continued its endless, silent, and now lonely way. It had been stripped, raped, and reduced to a dim shadow of its former glory.

It would spend the rest of its days traveling through the seas of space, lifeless, destined to travel forever with only the memory of the lives, the loves, and the glory which once flourished on its surface.

It had taken only a few cycles for billions of years of evolution and development to be erased. In a few moments, the Orb's life ceased. Nothing was left to testify to the miraculous evolution and the development of intelligence. There was only silence. Silence would forever haunt the surface of this now barren orb.

The precious cargo in the twenty-one, congested chemical rockets moved slowly through space. They were lifeboats, carrying cargo to a promised land. They were trying for an Orb considered to be a distant sister. This Orb too would pass the black hole but at a far enough distance that the effects would not be life threatening.

Nadia watched the devastation for the entire time. As her barren Home Orb continued on a now elongated orbit Nadia collapsed. She was physically and mentally exhausted.

She tried to contact Raulens and Milan. There was no answer. Had they been able to survive? If they had, for how long would they be able to do so, on the now barren Orb proceeding on its lonely way?

Nadia had no illusions. Without atmosphere, any life left on the planet had a very limited period in which to exist.

Throughout the catastrophic meeting with the void, the rockets had been moving toward the third Orb. With tears in her eyes, Nadia turned her telescope away from what had been her beloved home to the blue green world ahead.

It was a jewel, it was beautiful.

She had never been able to see it so clearly. She made a point of bringing each of her captains and showing them their goal. She also broadcast it through the computer systems so all could see their goal. In the following week all on board came to the main telescope to get a view of the third Orb firsthand. Nadia wanted to instill new hope.

Then the first radiation deaths occurred. The first death came at the end of seven work cycles. The five young persons, acting as doctors informed her many more were becoming sick. The radiation level had doubled. At the rate of increase they were experiencing the radiation level would be more than thirty times what they were currently experiencing.

Nadia quickly realized no one would survive to reach their destination.

Nadia was physically and mentally exhausted. There seemed to be no hope.

"You were chosen because you are our best bet at survival. You must think about your second plan and implement it," Lamins quietly reminded Nadia.

The blue jewel ahead of them could never be reached with their current radiation shielding. They must move out to areas of lower radiation. They must go out away from the sun. They would either have to find better shielding technology or find alternate sites to colonize.

"Thank you for being my conscience and reminding me that I must act," Nadia replied as she saw Lamins in a new light. He seemed to be rock. He reminded her of Raulens or Keren. She had never thought of Lamins in that way.

Nadia looked once more into the telescope and the Blue Orb. She ordered the ship cluster to turn around and go outward away from the sun. Then she called her captains together for a meeting.

"We have now lost six of our clan to radiation poisoning. Many more are sick. This is unusual for us. We normally recover from radiation exposure. Out here we have no place to hide to achieve this recovery. We must travel to areas of lower radiation. Though we thought the Blue Orb was our best option for colonization we must be able to survive the journey to reach

it. We must now go out to our alternate colonization sites."
Nadia said quietly to her team.

She encouraged debate about this decision. She wanted her captains to agree on the new strategy.

She knew immediate action ensured the survival group would recover. The recovery from radiation poisoning was something her species had developed over the millennium of their evolution. She needed to get the survivors to a lower radiation level where survival was possible.

She was encouraged by the discussion. No one questioned her decision, but they wondered if they could be successful in the quest for alternate colonization sites. Nadia pointed out eight potential sites. None of the choices were as good as the Blue Orb but all were farther away from the radiation currently threatening them.

"Please set up additional radiation shielding for those suffering the most. Use any materials necessary to create small individual radiation shelters," Nadia ordered.

She was sure she would need to use one of these shelters on a periodic basis.

Her rapid decision would be one that history would record as the first turning point that resulted in the survival of the Orbians.

<u>Chapter 11: Survivors</u>

The ships were now heading into the darkness and away from the Grand Orb. The radiation density was slowly dropping.

As the ships went outward away from the Grand Orb, the general health of the survivors improved almost immediately.

Nadia planned the outward journey to take them back by their Home Orb. She would utilize the Home Orb to accelerate her rockets to as high of a velocity as possible.

The outward journey would be across a vast distance.

This approach would also allow for a final check on the condition of the Home Orb. She had little hope of finding any survivors but she needed to see the condition of the home Orb one more time so she could accept the situation she was now in.

They had now been in space for thirty work cycles. As her cluster of ships passed the Home Orb, Nadia broadcast an inquiry to the surface on a continuous basis. She was not sure there would be any reply, but she was hoping for some survivors.

"I don't have much hope for a response, but we must continue to broadcast and to listen," she had instructed her crew.

They had all but given up hope when, to her amazement, a reply came back.

It was Keren! They had survived!

"We have survived the initial encounter. We are working to generate enough oxygen to sustain us over the long run. Milan has planted oxygen generating vines on every crevice and surface possible. We have enough food and water. We have not been able to contact any other groups on the Orb. What are you doing back?" Keren inquired.

"The radiation in toward the Third Orb is much stronger and deadlier than anticipated. Immediate deaths of seven survivors and the condition of the rest of the crew forced us to turn out toward the fifth Orb. We will go to the moons there to seek out new homes." Nadia replied.

Tears were streaming from her eyes as she completed the simple message.

"We have not been able to get out to the surface of the Orb. What is the condition of our home?" Keren inquired.

"There is nothing on the surface or in the Canyons. There is no Ocean, no visible water. The walls along the tops of the canyons are gone. No external structures are visible. If there is an atmosphere it is very thin. Tears are in my eyes as I speak. If I were coming for the first time to this Orb, I would think it was lifeless. We witnessed the Orb being stripped of its life. There is nothing visible at all on the surface." Nadia replied.

"I was afraid it would be that bad. The tunnel back to our survival area is blocked. We have not been able to get to the surface. The quakes and vibration threatened to destroy our survival chamber. Raulens has measured a change in the magnetic field and the orb must have lost at least ten percent of its mass. He now theorizes that this is our second encounter with the confluence. The first most likely destroyed the fifth orb and pieces of it hit our orb. This would explain why we have not been able to find the meteor or material that caused the initial damage to our Orb." Keren continued.

It was a relief for Keren to speak to someone outside of the survival chamber. He had been at a very low point in his emotions. Hearing Nadia immediately gave him new hope. He knew there was no atmosphere. He and two other survivors had gone out in the tunnel to determine if a way to the surface was open. They had to use spacesuits and carry their own oxygen.

The airtight design of the survival chamber had not been planned as such. The chamber was carved back into solid rock. It had only one entrance and it was only as wide as one of the boring machines. When it came time to design the doors, Raulens had specified what seemed to have been excessively thick walls and a vacuum chamber entrance. On the outer side of the vacuum chamber Raulens had designed a sliding ceramic barrier ten feet thick to further protect the entrance.

Keren told the construction crew to build whatever Raulens specified, and they did. At the time of confluence, the quakes, the bone rattling vibration, the noise caused all eyes to look at the entrance. Death was trying to break it down. Miraculously it held. A cheer by everyone inside had gone up when the rattling ended.

The power drive to move the barrier aside failed. However, Raulens had designed a manual retraction system. It took twelve cycles to slowly open the huge barrier door. The first few clicks were done very cautiously to make sure there were no unwanted materials trying to push in. They remained cautious and only opened the barrier enough to allow a suited person to get through.

Raulens supervised the building of an airtight folding seal to keep the precious air in the chamber from escaping.

Early on Milan recognized the need for a means to clean the air in the chamber. Her natural reaction was to review which plants would provide the most efficient conversion of the gases back to oxygen and nitrogen. She identified two plants.

It was a disappointment neither had food value, but their other capabilities caused her to energetically cultivate them. She and her recruits had planted them in every available space throughout the chamber. They needed the multi-frequency lights, water, and the minerals they found naturally in the surrounding rocks and soil.

Milan had also been responsible for ensuring there would be enough water for the survival containment. Here she followed Raulens approach and over designed the water chamber sizes. The water chamber was almost the same size as the living space. It was to the back and one level below the living space.

Milan had not wanted to get drowned in the event the quakes caused cracks to form. The amount of water now seemed inadequate.

Keren led the survivors. He was responsible for their selection, and he was naturally looked to as the leader. He had used his connection to the tunnel construction and Milan's and Raulens' money to construct the survival chamber.

He, Milan and Raulens together had selected the survivor candidates. They had decided on a family approach. There were only a few individuals without a family. They were the few who had been isolated doing the work to get the facility ready or who worked on the launch to the last possible moment. There were two hundred families and a total of one thousand survivors.

"Raulens sends his love and apology for under rating the radiation threat. Milan sends her love. And I am re-energized by your voice." Keren replied.

Nadia looked around the control room. Every individual was paying close attention. She saw hope in their faces as well as tears in their eyes.

"I will send periodic messages back to report on our progress. A survival group on our Home Orb is a blessing. My love to Milan and Raulens and best wishes to all" Nadia replied.

She was overjoyed. The contact was up lifting. It was the only positive event in recent times. She knew for most of the crew the return to their Orb only provided some closure to the pain of their loss. She was one of the lucky ones. It was a blessing the Evington family was in the survival group as well.

Nadia suspected Keren had been instrumental in the selection of Lamins as chief navigator. Nadia had come to realize the meaning of this arrangement and was pleased.

Lamins happily exchanged greetings with his parents. Then he turned the communication back to Nadia.

"We will be awaiting your reports. We in turn will send you, our status. Work is underway to improve our communication capability. We need to clear a path through the tunnel to the surface. We will then aim our antennas in your direction. This work will take some time. Space suits are now required outside of our survival containment. You will know immediately of our success." Keren replied.

There was no more to say. The crews in space now guided their combined rocket structure around what had been their Home Orb.

The sling around the Orb provided the desired additional velocity. Lamins plotted out the new course to the fifth Orb.

"We are leaving what is left of our Home Orb and the few survivors and will be looking for our new home. Meanwhile we will reconfigure our current home into a system that has the gravity we need," Nadia announced to the captains of the ships.

She and most of the rest of the crew had learned to live with nausea. The crew had become quite good at floating around the interior of the structure and doing the required work. The normal bodily functions were a challenge to manage but everyone seemed to have learned to manage these personal challenges.

Re-establishing gravity and a way to sustain the crew over a prolonged period became the immediate priority.

The gardens had to begin producing food. The learning of Milan's oxygen generating plants was very useful. Additional growing areas along all passageways was now in the planning.

The captains of each rocket were reorganized into a planning, coordination, and supervisory team. They were charged with preparing for a long stay in space and a long journey through the Orbital system.

The journey to the fifth Orb would take at least two of their Home Orb cycles. Once at the fifth Orb, Nadia expected it would take a full Orb cycle to analyze the situation and prepare for the colonization.

Small construction teams began modifying each rocket to the two-level design planned for the rotating configuration. The levels ran the length of each rocket. The outer part of the wheel would be gardens and the inner level would be living and workspace.

The design was reviewed with the planning board. Every person was put to work on getting the transformation of the rockets into a spinning wheel done quickly.

The center section was built first. The central rocket in the current arrangement was the starting point. This was built by using the last rocket sent up by Raulens. It was the longest of all the rockets and provided the most space. In the long term it would serve as storage, work centers and be the main air scrubbing and water recycle center. The nose and engine sections of the rocket were removed. An inward concave cap was put in on each end. Ten floors were installed.

Nadia had all personnel and support materials temporarily moved into this central rocket.

It was a very tight fit. Double bunking was the norm.

"It's lucky we are a species that enjoys close spaces," Lamins joked when he saw how tight the arrangement turned out to be.

No one complained.

Each rocket had been designed and marked to fit a specific location.

The center rocket sections were the easiest to modify and put into place. Since the rockets built in the launch tubes in Ulm were larger in diameter than those built in the other canyons they were designated as the spokes that radiated out from the vertical center section. Five of the rockets became the spokes.

The five were vertical work areas with very weak outward centrifugal pull. This pull would be about a third of the force of normal gravity. These would be storage and work areas. Each would be utilized for a different function. The low gravitational force would make it easier to manipulate heavy materials and equipment. Unlike the center rocket, the floors in these sections ran the length of the rockets. The rockets were all brought together in a spoke hub connection point.

There was a top and bottom rim around the central rocket. Here each spoke was terminated creating a hallway around the outside of the central rocket. At this level traffic could go around the exterior portion of the hallway or directly through the core. The vertical rocket sections were positioned between each of the spokes as close to the center as possible. Each of the five vertical rocket sections opened into the circular hallway.

Joining the radial spoke to the smaller diameter T section took as much time as doing all the rest of the interior work. The connection pieces had been made before launch, but they were still hard to manipulate and to weld. The welds had to be done from both the inside and the outside of the hull. Then each of the ceramic layers needed to be joined and the gap spaces filled. The crew managing their assembly decided to make the primary welds but defer the multiple layer construction until after the ship was rotating.

The first T section was outfitted and put into place. The permanent residents for this section were identified and the first to move in. They would have more room and only needed to make their move once. However, each of them still had a double bunk mate. This move opened up the space in the central rocket and made it more livable.

The wheel began its rotation after the first T section was completed. The initial rotation produced thirty percent of the pull of gravity. This allowed the first garden to start up and the first crop was planted. The oxygen bearing plants were started along the radial spoke.

Even this lower gravity was a much better living environment for the crew. It also allowed for a slow readjustment to gravity that all the crew would need to go through.

"The gradual return to full gravity will make it easier for the crew to readjust," Nadia commented as she and Lamins inspect the first section. "The timing of getting the system fully functional will be about right for this readjustment she concluded."

The additional sections were scheduled to be added in a balanced fashion. The radial spokes were all immediately attached to the central core. The T sections were cut to the marked angles and sealed on each end. One by one the end T sections were moved into position and welded. The decision to only weld the outside layer greatly increased the speed of construction.

After the third T section was in place the crew once again was moved in. The end of double bunking was celebrated as was the increase of the centrifugal force to sixty per cent of gravity.

Each rocket needed to be brought into position. The excess sections removed. The angles for each joint had previously been determined and the ends of each rocket had been designed to easily remove the unneeded sections. The task was to join each section to its designated mating rocket. All extra materials were brought to the center workshops for recycling. All this material was considered valuable and would be processed for later use.

The construction became more challenging as the rotation was increased. The final T sections and the sections connecting the T's to each other now were moved into position using cables. Each section was moved out beyond the diameter of the wheel so they could be properly oriented and then pulled slowly back into position. The section joints were designed to snap together and lock.

The seal welding was the only work needing to be done by hand. Welding occupied eighty per cent of those who were putting the wheel together. Once in place each section was quickly spot welded from both the interior and exterior of the joint.

Once the last section went in, the rotation of the ship would be increased to match the gravitational force of their Home Orb.

Managing this transition and ensuring the safety and the survival of everyone was a major effort. Nadia and her captains had their hands full. Everyone on the crew was given a task. Half of the crew was charged with supporting those doing the work.

About a third of the crew was old enough and skilled enough to help with the building of the rotating wheel. Nadia was relieved that there were only a few accidents but no fatalities.

Everyone was still recovering from the shock of the confluence. Nadia ensured each Captain spent an hour each period with his or her crew to discuss any issues, feelings, and reaction to the goals for the journey.

The inability to make the journey to the third orb had weighed most heavily on Nadia. She understood the negative impact it had on their chances of long-term survival. There were no other sites with as high of a potential as the third Orb.

These daily discussion sessions were duplicated with the Captains and Nadia. She worked with them to ensure they too were working through their problems, grief, and shock.

She herself shared her problems with Lamins. The two of them had become exceptionally close. She knew she was lucky to have found such a steadying partner. All their lives they had been friends and it was a luxury to share similar memories. She suspected Keren had a hand in Lamins being the Chief Navigator. If possible, she would thank him later.

Nadia continued sending weekly progress reports to her Home Orb. She hoped the survivors there were making progress in re-establishing themselves. Knowing that there were survivors helped everyone on the ships but especially helped her.

The daily routine and work seemed to go on forever. After almost a full rotational period all the major work on the ship was complete. The complex joints at the T's were the only remaining work of completing the fundamental structure of the ship.

A contest was held to select a name for their ship. Nadia was surprised at the number of those suggesting, Confluence. Several other names came up but when the names were put up for a vote, Confluence was chosen by a large majority.

Ron Mueller

Chapter 12: Regaining a foothold

The clearing of a way out to the edge of the canyon was challenging the capability of the survivors on the Home Orb. The way was blocked by a mix of twisted, interwoven building materials, rail tracks, vehicles, and even a train engine.

The limited number of suits kept the work party small. The size of the work parties was not an issue since the workspace was so tight. The exoskeletons proved to be invaluable in providing the lifting and physical strength needed to dig through and move the material blocking the way out. Every foot of progress was a fight trying to untangle the interwoven refuse. Keren figured the force of the rushing water had forcefully hurled the material into the tunnel.

The recovered materials were all considered extremely valuable. Everyone knew that their long term survival would depend on much of the materials. They were pulled out and taken back to the survival enclosure or to an empty chamber located farther into the tunnel.

The rubble was moved back into the tunnel and separated as much as possible. Later this rubble might also prove to be valuable.

The outward digging continued in as straight a line as possible but several large and currently immovable objects, like the train engine caused the excavation to twist and turn as it progressed. It all seemed to be an insane mix of debris.

The bodies mixed in with the rubble were more disturbing than gruesome. The current lack of air caused the decomposition to be very slow. Some bodies looked to have just passed away. This aspect almost always caused those finding a body to check for life. Most of those found had documentation identifying who they were.

The issue of what to do with the deceased had not been addressed by the survivors. The bodies were handled with respect and moved to a large, excavated room far back in the tunnel. It became an open burial site. Two of the religious leaders were in charge of the burial services. At the end of the work cycle, several individuals would don space suits and exoskeletons and along with several other witnesses perform the burials. The bodies were wrapped and were laid out side by side in long rows.

Every work cycle uncovered a least a dozen victims. This slowed down the digging significantly, but no one complained. Everyone was greatly saddened and affected by each new body found.

A cheer went up when the digging broke through to the main outer tunnel. This was followed by total silence as the entire team gathered to look in both directions. The tunnel was eerily empty. There were a few foundational structures, but the waters had washed all signs of the rail system and all residential structures out of existence. There was nothing where millions had once lived. Many had come to the tunnels with the thought of it being a safe haven from the Confluence. Instead, it placed them in the direct path of the force of the supersonic water flow. The rail system had become one of the main paths for the waters to move from one canyon to another. Nothing had survived the direct impact of this flow.

Having reached the main tunnel, three major efforts were undertaken in parallel. One exploratory team was sent to Ulm to examine the city and see if there were any survivors. They took with them a special four wheeled cart. It was an air chamber and could hold up to six beings. The team would be looking for survivors and was prepared to bring them back. They were also to evaluate the condition of the city and determine if there was any way to utilize the facilities and materials. A second exploratory team was sent in the other direction toward New Ulm with the same mission.

Keren was in charge of the third team. It would go to the surface and set up a communication antenna capable of reaching the survivors out in space. This team was to go up an elevator shaft to the surface.

It quickly became clear climbing up in their space gear would be impossible.

This elevator shaft had survived the rush of the water because the top cap that sealed the shaft had held. The water did not tear it out.

Keren had the team use the emergency rescue release to lower the still existing elevator. It originally operated on locally mounted electric motor drives. These were now inoperable. However, the team was able to set up a manually driven gear system that would slowly lift them to the surface.

The trip up would take several cycles. The elevator platform was transformed into an airtight chamber. This arrangement freed the team to manually work the lifting gear. It took two of them at a time to turn the hand operated wheel attached to the gearing system.

Keren quickly became frustrated with the slow progress. He decided they would need to set up some sort of power system.

The cabling for the antenna was on a reel. It was the main weight being lifted toward the surface. One end was attached at the tunnel level and periodically Keren would attach the cable to a rail in the corner of the elevator shaft. The going got easier as the cable was slowly unreeled. At the end of three cycles, they reached the surface. There had never been much out at this level. However, it had never been this clear of loose stone and rubble. The landscape was totally bare.

"Nadia was right, there is nothing left of any of our handiwork. The surface has been stripped bare," Keren commented as the team unloaded their gear.

The team pulled out the dish antenna and carried it to a nearby area of pure rock. There they anchored the base to the rock with power rivets. They pointed the antenna toward the location Raulens had predicted the fifth planet would be.

The antenna was outfitted with a small battery driven motor that would allow rotating and tilting commands to be executed. The control center was located in the survival chamber.

"Time to check out the controls to this antenna," Keren talked into his portable communication headset.

"Ok, I am going to move the antenna through its entire range to ensure it is working as planned," Milan replied.

Once the antenna was checked and once again pointing to where they had calculated Nadia would be, Keren sent out the first message.

"We have made it to the surface of our Orb. Our antenna is in place, and we send you greetings. We thank you for naming the moons to be colonized after us. We feel honored. We are all well and continue to make progress. Hope all is well with you. Please send confirmation of receiving this message.

Keren had his team pack up the equipment and began the journey down to the survival chamber.

The Ulm exploratory team lead by Raulens walked along the tunnel toward the city. Their trip was planned for three to five cycles in duration. They would spend the nights in the cart they were pulling. They estimated it would take them a full cycle to reach the city. Once there they would make an initial assessment and decide how to proceed.

The first location was to be the food production facilities. Any packaged food would be gathered and brought back. They would catalogue the amounts and quantities. Much of the packaged food would last for years. This would ensure that food would not be an issue to the survivors.

The team also carried a long list of materials needed for production of the many tools and implements needed to sustain themselves. There would be no shortage of any of them if the facilities had survived the Confluence.

Raulens was amazed at how little he could recognize. He was now thirty-five cycles of age. He was the old person of the group. He had been around for much of the modernization of Ulm. What he did not see kept him off balance. When they reached the city, he was once again shocked.

The waters from the Ocean had come in from outside and up the elevator shafts. The elevators traveling to the surface were totally stripped. Those elevators leading to the rail tunnels were totally stripped. These elevators had been subject to the full force of the supersonic water flow and had been blown clear. The secondary elevators to various manufacturing or living levels seemed to have been randomly affected. There were a few with little or no damage. The only problem with them was the need for power. The water had taken the route of least resistance. It had devastated these routes and usually scrubbed them clean.

Most tunnels leading back to the manufacturing levels were designed with blocking gates. These had been closed prior to the Confluence. Most had held. The water took the path of least resistance and flowed along the rail tunnel.

Raulens decided to check the chambers first. He was not prepared for what he found beyond the gates. There were bodies for as far as his light cast its glow. They looked to be asleep. His team was silent as they took in the scene. They checked a few of the bodies and called out in hopes of finding someone alive. There was no response. They closed the gate and went to the next one only to find the same scene. They repeated their call. Then they closed the gates.

None of his team wanted to go into the chambers that were now the tomb for so many of their dead.

Raulens remembered a private entrance Milan had taken him through. He took his team there. When they opened the smaller blocking gate, the hall was empty. They proceeded along the hall to the main interior garden area. The plants appeared to have survived and were still doing well. There were a few dead bodies, but this had not been a gathering place for the masses. They went through the garden area to the food processing plant and out to the storage area. They found a vast amount of processed vegetables and fruits. They decided to take this first load and then take one more exploratory trip to determine how they would proceed the next time they came back.

The biggest problem facing them was how to bury all the dead. Potentially there were hundreds of thousands to millions in the various tunnels. No one could think of any way to handle so many dead Orbians.

"We will let them sleep where they died. Each area will become their grave," Raulens made an unsolicited comment to his team.

The team said nothing, but they all nodded their heads in agreement.

The team going to New Ulm pulled a similar cart and was just as shocked as the team going in the opposite direction toward Ulm. The waters had come down the tunnel from Ulm toward New Ulm. It had also proceeded over the mantle. It had cleaned everything out of the tunnel. What it had carried over the mantle was an unknown.

New Ulm was not as developed as Ulm. It was half the size of Ulm and had been carved into the mantle in a more economical way than the construction of Ulm. The difference was now readily apparent. Most of New Ulm had been cleared by the force of the water gushing through the tunnels. This team did not find the multitude of bodies.

They found very little overall.

There would be tremendous amounts of material that would be available for salvage. They did find bodies in the thousands. These seemed to have been randomly dropped across the city. There seemed to be no survivors.

They were about ready to leave when they heard a banging. They followed the sound to a large tunnel barrier doorway. The banging seemed to be coming from the other side. They banged on their side of the door. The banging increased in intensity. There was a service door at the corner of the barrier gate. They took their cart and sealed it to the doorway prior to opening the door.

Two emaciated youngsters stepped back in fright. The team, in their space suits and exoskeleton must have been a fearsome sight. The team leader experimentally opened his space suit. He found a very weak but breathable atmosphere. He asked about other survivors. The two explained they had been alone for about three cycles. The others had passed away as the oxygen in the tunnel slowly escaped.

It became clear to the team leader he would not be able to keep his suit open. He escorted the two into the cart and then resealed his suit.

The team fed the two surviving youngsters. The female was four and her brother five cycles in age. They had survived because they were little and required less oxygen. After giving them food and water, the team questioned the two about the potential of any other survivors. There had been only a handful of people who had come to one of the factory isolation chambers. Her father had worked in this chamber and knew it could be sealed. He had planned to survive the confluence and had. The devastation of the planet was beyond what he had planned for. He and his family slowly ran out of food and air. The two youngsters had only survived because this section of the city had miraculously held the air in for such a long period.

The team found no other survivors. They located the isolation chamber the youngsters had described and verified no one was alive. They buried the parents. There was an entire city to investigate but travel up the elevators would be a challenge. They decided to return to their survival chamber with the two youngsters. The next team would need to come prepared to go up the elevator shafts if they were to explore the city.

Keren, Raulens, Milan and the rest discussed the situation. They had survived and now they had to reconstruct and build on their survival. They were looking at a monumental and perhaps impossible re-establishment of their society. They agreed that they would go forward one cycle at a time.

<u>Chapter 13: First Colonies</u>

The outer orbs were all large with overwhelming gravitational forces. This made them unsuitable for colonization. Their moons were the target. The next Orb was a giant with four potential moons. These had been studied and analyzed before the survival launch. Nadia was glad she had pushed her team do this analysis. Now she used the onboard telescope to get an even better view. She had each potential site more thoroughly analyzed.

Nadia named the highest potential moons after her immediate family. She sent a message back to her Home Orb to let them know. She did not expect an answer because the radio signal from the Home Orb had been very weak as they went past. As promised, she had sent work cycle reports for the past Orbian cycle back to Keren. It helped her and she hoped he was receiving the messages and hoped it would help the family.

Nadia was pessimistic about the chances of her family's survival. She knew her family would not let her know if they were facing death. She also knew the power of their combined capability and hoped it was sufficient to the challenge facing them.

She had to believe they would succeed. It drove her to create success with her responsibility.

The analysis team Nadia established on the Confluence observed and thoroughly analyzed each of the many object's circling the giant orb they were approaching. They carefully studied each of the selected moons. There were close to one hundred orbiting objects but only three were suitable. There was an advantage to having three colonies so close together. They would not have the capability to help each other but they would be able to easily communicate. This in itself made an enormous difference.

Milan was the smallest and the moon closest to the giant orb. It was just inside the magnetic field of the giant. Sixty percent smaller than Raulens but with an ice covered, salty ocean it appeared habitable. It had a metallic core and a rocky mantle. Huge cracks in the ice indicated the liquid below the ice regularly expanded. Situating the colony would be a challenge. The Milan colonization team thoroughly studied their new home.

The vertical temperature differential found in the salty ocean could be harnessed to provide the colony with an energy source. It could be used to power the heating system that would be required. This would be critical for long term survival. Milan might even have its own life forms in the depth of the ocean. Milan's circumference was half and its' mass only eight percent of their Home Orb. The gravitational pull was correspondingly weaker as well. One key advantage was it had the best radiation shielding of selected moons.

Raulens was the largest moon. Its circumference was only thirty percent less than their Home Orb, but its mass was significantly less. It did have a very thin atmosphere and constituent gases would allow for the generation of breathable air.

It appeared to have a metallic core and a rock mantle surrounding the core. The entire surface was covered by a very thick layer of water ice. There were huge rocks mixed in the ice layers.

The colony would be located by one of these huge floating rocks. The extremely low temperature would also be a challenge. Once again, the temperature differential in the ice covering from the upper layers to the lower layers was enough to establish a power generation system. The Raulens colonization team thoroughly studied their new home.

If successful, one could envision a day when the two colonies would establish transport and trade. This at least was the rational Nadia and Lamins shared with each other.

Nadia had a large sense of guilt to ask those going down to the moons to do so.

The size of Keren made it a target but once the analysis came in it became questionable about its suitability. It traveled the outermost orbit of the three and it had the lowest density of the three satellites. It appeared to have a metallic core and a smaller thinner mantle. It was totally covered with a shell of ice. The atmosphere was a thick carbon monoxide. It appeared the surface had never experienced resurfacing. This implied a dead or inactive world.

The technical understanding of the targets for colonization greatly increased as the Confluence studied them on a shadowing journey around the giant.

What bothered Nadia the most was once a colony group descended to the surface, she had no way to rescue them. Colonization was a one-way trip. Survival on the surface would need to be achievable and sustainable by those on the surface. Only limited additional aid could be provided.

"Each colonization team member has a choice. You do not need to go if you have any doubts. We will accept your decision. Once you are down on the surface, it will be impossible for us to rescue you. Your survival will be in your hands. You will need to work together to achieve a survival level," Nadia commented to the colonization teams.

Nadia and the entire crew of the Confluence was surprised but overjoyed at the clear message from their Home Orb. It came in weak but clear. Nadia broadcast the message to the crew and a cheer could be heard throughout the ship. It was so uplifting to hear of the success of the survivors back on their Home Orb.

"You are the proud designers and sponsors of a spaceship called Confluence. It now spins and generates one gravitational pull.

We have oxygen bearing plants covering the inside walls of almost every surface and our gardens are in full production. Thank you, Milan, for giving us this gift.

We were able to assemble this complicated vessel because of the snap together design. The radiation shielding is working well. Thank you, Raulens.

And I have an excellent partner as a senior navigator. Thank you, Keren.

We on the Confluence are doing well. We have now been out more than a full Orbian cycle. The original intention was a modest one third of a cycle. We are close to arriving at our initial destination. Your ability to send us your message has raised our hopes; thank you.

Have you received our previous reports?" Nadia replied.

It became apparent to Nadia and Lamins that the Confluence would become a permanent home for a part of the survivors.

How many would stay with the vessel was unclear. The number would depend on the number volunteering to try and colonize the selected orbs. There could be up to eight colonies spread across the four outer Orbs.

Three colony groups were identified, and volunteers came forward and were grouped according to desire and established personal associations. Nadia could only wonder how she would have acted at the young age of most of the volunteers. True bravery was on display by all of them.

Each group identified and staffed the various roles. They then began to practice their initial colonization actions. First, they needed to establish their living area. Each colony had one of the Captains as the leader and three additional team leaders. They would form the governing body and would lead four separate activities; camp establishment; area surveillance; internal construction and overall support.

The three groups worked and practiced for the entire rotation around the giant orb.

Nadia and Lamins spent an hour a day with each of the three leadership teams of these groups. The three colonies would be established in sequence. The team descending to Raulens would be first. The team descending to Milan would be second. The third team would descend to Keren only after a closer re-examination of the conditions when the Confluence got closer to it.

The Confluence would stay in orbit for at least a half of their Home Orb cycle while the colonies established themselves. It would remain near Keren during this time. This proximity would aid in the re-evaluation of it as a colonization site.

There were to be five hundred in each colony. Each colony would take their portion of the gardens. The oxygen generation chambers were to be sent down first. Once established and proved to be working, a small contingent of the camp establishment team would descend and assemble a section of the living quarters. Establishing an energy generation source was the next critical factor. Once the source of energy was validated, the remainder of the colony would descend in an orchestrated sequence. The sequence was designed to balance the work to establish the compound and its exterior with the work to establish the interior living quarters and the setup of the maintenance equipment.

The gardens were the most important aspect of colony establishment.

The extra materials and equipment, Raulens had sent up on the last and twenty first rocket, now became very valuable.

The machine shop on board was busy making a variety of equipment from hammers, to cook stoves, to chairs.

The electronics was reconfigured to provide surface communication as well as communication with the Confluence.

The material for the living quarters came from sections of the center of the Confluence. Eventually the Confluence would be totally consumed if all parties were to go down to some satellite.

Once each colony was stabilized, the Confluence would proceed outward to the next orb. The astronomy team found at least one potential colonization site circling the next orb.

One small team was established to do a more in-depth study of the objects circling the next Orb beyond the next orb but the distance out to it was greater than what they had come so far. Analysis would require more information than they could obtain at this distance. The best they could currently accomplish was an orbital mapping.

Study of the first three selected colonization sites continued. A total orb mapping was being done and studied in detail. The leaders for each colonization group studied the maps and all the information about their destination. Selection of the actual colonization site on the surface would require careful study. Close proximity to minerals and rock formations allowing excavation for living space made a site desirable. ice would be the main building material. The living quarters were designed to be cut out of the ice.

The cold on all these colony sites made the effort more perilous. The temperature would be the most difficult element to overcome. A means of insulating and heating would need to be established. Insulation material was the most important item for each colony.

The science team came up with an innovative approach. The gases in the site's atmosphere would serve to insulate the thin structures making up the living quarters. These gases would be trapped between the walls of the compound and would essentially act as a total insulation barrier. This provided the maximum insulation and would save on materials.

The source of energy and the technology to harness it was the next challenge. Drilling the deep well in which to lower thermal tubes required both power and a way to dispose of the material being drilled.

Nadia and Lamins spent many hours reviewing the details of the planned colonies. It was becoming clearer to them these colonies were going to be very high-risk efforts. Except for the captains and their mates, the remaining members were children. Both shared their feelings of guilt and also of despair with each other. They could not, however, see any other option. They had to try to establish the colonies.

Each colony was being deployed into the most perilous conditions either of them could imagine. Once on the surface the colony could request additional help or materials.

The response of the Confluence would need to be measured. It was this aspect that bothered Nadia the most. She hoped she would not be asked to make the choice on the potential survival of one group and the threat of shortchanging another one.

The rotational period of the moons was a critical learning. Milan was closest to the gigantic sixth orb. It was roughly 700,000 kilometers from the giant and made the trip around it in roughly three and a half Orbian cycles. Raulens was roughly 1,000,000 kilometers out and made the trip around in a little over seven Orbian cycles. Keren was almost twice as far out as Raulens at roughly 1,800,000 kilometers and made the trip around in 16.7 Orbian cycles.

Milan seemed to be the most active and seemed to be a world with an ocean of salt water below a tremendously thick layer of ice. Raulens was extremely cold, but it had a thin oxygen layer. Keren was the most interesting. Its mantel was heavily marked by the objects bombarding it through the millennium. This indicated it had not had any active mantle movement for billions of cycles and it had a large amount of Carbon Dioxide.

On board the Confluence they still kept time based on their Home Orb cycle. It took two cycles for the first two colonies to get down on the surface and get set up. Each site had been located to optimize the colonies chances at survival. In all cases the trips down had been safely accomplished. Each had initial set up challenges but slowly seemed to overcome them.

Neither colony asked for any additional help.

After study and analysis, the colonization of Keren was abandoned. There were too many barriers to overcome. Its dramatically longer journey around the giant orb also put it out of communication with the other orbs for prolonged periods of time. Periods that represented half a lifetime for the Orbians.

Nadia and the remaining members of the Confluence readjusted the design of the ship's interior. Additional space was allocated to growing more food. Nadia and her team had designed a way to capture space dust and materials by taking the Confluence through a particle area at the same velocity as the particles. As the Confluence rotated it pulled the particles into the center. The captured materials proved to be invaluable.

It was a source of water, oxygen, and materials for the gardens. During the two periods circling the giant planet the Confluence doubled the food production capacity. Nadia sent the two colonies all the additional food. She made sure each colony had every bit of food and extra materials possible.

The collection of the materials also provided the basis for the segregation of key minerals. This was an effort Nadia developed with an eye to the future. The Confluence would need to obtain the minerals and materials to achieve a self-sufficient survival level. She had come to the realization the Confluence would need to be maintained for a dramatically longer time period than originally planned.

She started a ship expansion team to study how to make the Confluence a stronger and bigger ship.

The colonies seemed to have gotten a good start. All had been able to set up their living areas and their gardens were in production. They were actively establishing the resources to secure their future survival.

It was time to move out to the next Orb and determine if another colony would be set up there. The distance and the time to reach this next potential site would be measured in multiple Orbian cycles. They would be in transit for at least four Orbian cycles.

Nadia contacted each of the colonies and bid them good luck.

"The Confluence is on its way to the next colonization site. Our hopes are with you. May you fare well," Nadia sent her message to both colonies.

The Confluence planned to return but it would be gone for at least eight to twelve cycles. They would keep in touch with each colony and send them periodic updates of the journey.

Both colonies asked that she send them any songs she might write. This last was a surprise to her. She had remained a singing star to her crew. Her songs were now about their journey, the survivors back on the Home Orb and the future.

Chapter 14: Home Orb Re-colonization

Finding two survivors at New Ulm was cause for an immediate return to each of the two cities. Keren recalled the city plans for Ulm were stored in the magistrate's office area. This was in the government plaza located at the thirtieth level. The first priority was to get the plans and identify potential survival chambers. Each survival potential would be visited on the next trip to the cities.

A simple battery powered L lift was designed to carry one exoskeleton suited individual. Each of the team carried their own L lift. The L lift used the elevator cable as the track and slowly lifted the rider. On return to the city, Keren located an elevator leading to the thirtieth level. This elevator came within a block of the magistrate's office. The team was glad there were no bodies at this level. They had been overwhelmed by their initial find at the rail level.

They carefully made their way to the magistrate's office. There was an eerie feeling to this trip. Ulm was so quiet and so empty. What would have once been busy walkways and trams were now silent and empty.

It took the team most of a cycle to locate the desired city plans. These plans were still on transparent plastic film. This was actually a piece of good luck. If they had been entered into the computer system, they may not have been retrievable.

A flashlight provided the back lighting needed to read the various plans. They found three potential survival chambers on the thirtieth level. They needed such a location to establish a home base from which they could explore the other potential sites.

The closest building was a bank. The chamber was the bank vault. The team had no way to enter this vault. They hammered on the outside of the vault door. There was no response. The team was relieved. They had wondered what they would have done if someone hammered back.

The next chamber was a huge refrigeration unit at the edge of the level. They approached the unit and noted there were three doors, and each had small windows. They tried to look in, but the windows had been covered by a steel plate. They hammered on the door and were shocked when there was a response.

They had come equipped for just such a situation but were still taken by surprise. The mere fact of survivors was a point of celebration.

They immediately set up their inflatable flexible pressure chamber. Keren, less the exoskeleton stood in the bladder. The bladder was pressurized. He then tried to open the door. He gave the familiar knock used to indicate a friend at the door. The door cracked open ever so little. When those inside realized there was pressure on the other side of the door it opened the rest of the way.

Keren stepped in and took off the helmet of his pressure suit. He looked around at the throng of people. There were at least thirty in the group. They seemed in good health. He introduced himself and was surprised when someone in the group commented he was glad that he had voted for him at the last election.

"Glad to see my vote counted," was the glib comment.

The leader or spokesperson for the group asked what the situation was outside. Keren informed the group that he came from a chamber where one thousand had survived. He let them know his team was just beginning a search for survivors and they were the first to be found. He discussed the arrangements to transport the thirty people back at the end of the fifth work cycle.

"Please send the first message back to the survival colony. This will be good news to those supporting us." Keren said as he gave the leader the small battery powered transmitter-receiver radio.

The radio was able to communicate back to the survival chamber via a local relay station they had set up down at the rail level.

The people in the room were all in great spirits as Keren said goodbye, put on his helmet, and exited through the door. He heard it close behind him. He then signaled to have the bladder depressurized.

The team went to the final location on the thirtieth floor. There was no one at this last location. They set up camp and pressurized the chamber. The rest of the cycle was spent identifying and prioritizing the order of their search for survivors. There were roughly two hundred possible sites.

Out of the two hundred sites they prioritized and searched they found another six hundred and sixteen survivors.

The search took almost thirty Central Orb cycles.

Finding the survivors was uplifting but the team found millions more that had died of suffocation.

There was no way the survivors could handle all the dead. The areas of the city where most of the dead were located were closed off. There were millions of bodies in the tunnels of Ulm.

The entire population of the survival group was involved in evaluating what to do. They decided to use several of the long tunnels for burial mausoleums.

The survivors that were found were transported back to the survival compound and integrated into the work to reclaim a foot hold on their Orb. The work ahead would keep everyone occupied.

Eventually they would need to reconcile their survival with the millions of dead. But first they had to ensure their continued survival.

The teams working in Ulm and New Ulm used carts to move the bodies into several of the main tunnels designated to be mausoleums. With the minimal atmosphere that now existed on the Orb, there was little decomposition of the bodies.

The decision to organize and move the bodies into the tunnels was also based on the fact that there were only a few exoskeletons and spacesuits available. The effort to respectfully put the bodies to rest took almost a full Central Orb cycle. To speed the handling of the dead three teams were designated to do the work in each city. The teams located and outfitted several pressurize chambers in key levels in both cities.

The three teams went through each city in a planned order. There were a limited number of carts available to be used to move the bodies. The three teams worked around the clock. One team would be in a rest period. One team recorded the names of those being moved to their resting place. The third team moved the bodies. The teams worked for seven work cycles. They then returned to the survival chamber for two work cycles. This work went on until the city was cleared.

There were still additional bodies, but these would continue to be found in the coming work cycles as the recovery continued.

In all the time of moving bodies to the selected tunnels only five more live beings were found. There were no additional survivors in Ulm or New Ulm. They hoped there were some in the other canyons, but they doubted there were any. The construction of those cities had taken a much more linear approach and would have been destroyed even more than New Ulm.

The survivors planned on a wider sweep once they had the first two cities in control.

The work of laying the millions of dead to rest exhausted the survivors and taxed their emotions. Most of those found were strangers to the survivors. A few were good friends. Many were just acquaintances. They were all dead. Seeing so many of their kind dead was devastating and a huge emotional drain.

Raulens and Milan spent a great deal of time holding counseling sessions to discuss their survival and the need for everyone to look forward to a new tomorrow.

Keren would always wonder if more should or could have been done to create additional survival chambers. Hindsight was of no value, and he concentrated on what to do for the future.

The messages of progress coming from Nadia on a consistent basis gave all the survivors a basis for hope.

Her messages were consumed and listened to multiple times. Her voice and new songs were constantly being listened to. She was by far the most inspirational one of all of them.

Chapter 15: Third Colony

The embrace of the void and darkness surrounding the Confluence could not penetrate into the glow and high energy level those on board experienced. Everyone had the surreal experience of enjoying an environment that seemed to warmly embrace them. The horror and pain of their loss of all those on their Home Orb seemed to be what was not real.

The trip out to the third colony would take at least one and a half Orbian cycles. During this time daily communications and updates were maintained with the first two colonies.

The Confluence team worked on the reconfiguration of the vessel from the loss of materials to the first two colonies and it prepared for the removal of material for the third colony. It was clear to Lamens that a ship design team was needed. He established this with a view to the long-term life on the Confluence.

Nadia consistently sent messages and reports back to the Home Orb. She periodically received confirmation of these messages. She shared all the information with those on the Confluence and those at the two colonies. She knew the flow of information among the survivors provided a significant level of hope.

Nadia guided the analysis of the objects orbiting the next giant orb. There was only one moon with the promise of supporting a colony. It was almost as large as Raulens. Nadia asked Lamins to name the moon to be colonized.

Lamins named it Hope.

He hoped it would be a place where life could be sustained.

Hope turned out to be as cold and foreboding as the other moons. It was clear there would be no warm worlds for them to colonize.

Hope was encased in a thick, hazy atmosphere. The surface temperature was even colder than the previous two colony sites. There was a surface continent surrounded by liquid. The liquid appeared to be similar to a combustible fuel found on their Home Orb.

The atmosphere on Hope was mostly nitrogen but had high percentages of methane and ethane. Making breathable air would not be a major obstacle. Moving about would require support and a supply of self-contained air. Having sufficient energy would not be the obstacle.

The obstacle on Hope was the atmospheric pressure. It was two hundred percent greater than on their Home Orb. Movement on the surface would only be possible in a rigid enclosure that maintained the required pressure.

The Confluence's "engineering" team designed and built surface work boxes or vehicles to facilitate the construction of a living space. These vehicles were designed to allow physical work to be done from the inside lower pressured containment. This meant a tight seal had to be maintained. Safety backups were designed into the containment vessels.

The makeup of the liquid "ocean" was still being studied but is seemed to hold the potential for life. This was seen as positive. No one expected there to be life as they knew or understood it, but this likelihood provided more confidence the colony would figure out how to harness this resource.

The travel time out was barely sufficient for the colony members to prepare. They organized in the same manner as the other two colonies. Their plans were to establish the colony underground. The higher locations bordering the sea were the primary sites. The colony would locate their facility underground in the rock.

The boring would be straight down for at least a thousand feet. The work to establish the colony would take twice the time used by the previous colonies. Boring through rock was slower and more labor intensive than the boring done into the ice on Raulens and Milan.

Once at the desired depth, the excavation would be continued horizontally out from the vertical bore hole.

The excavated material would all need to be lifted to the surface. This material would be utilized to create a containment structure to be a barrier against the external conditions and to create a location for the creation, filtering, and processing of the air required to support the colonist.

This surface structure would also be where the fuel to provide energy would be processed. It would be filtered from the sea and condensed to a useable strength.

Unlike Raulens and Milan where the energy was generated from a thermal gradient, the energy on Hope would be generated by combustion.

The Confluence team designed and built a series of small engines and turbines to convert the combustion energy into electrical power.

The combustion processes would all take place on the surface. Only electrical energy would be utilized down in the excavated living spaces.

Like the other colonies the means to be self-supporting was studied carefully and everything possible was developed and made available.

The Confluence would lose its third garden section. It however it would not lose any of the sections needed for housing as had been used on the first two colonies.

The crew of the Confluence spent the majority of their transit time reconfiguring the structure. The center sections were now either with one of the first two colonies or getting outfitted to go down to the third colony. Only two T sections remained as originally configured. The other three T section materials had been removed to provide housing and gardens to the colonists. The central storage and the circular hall were now comprised of only the central rocket. The overall structural integrity was sound, and the balance of the Confluence's structure maintained.

This reduction in space was not noticeable since there had also been a reduction in the number of the crew. The reduction in energy use was noticeable.

The Confluence had never been designed to remain in space for very long. Now after six and a half cycles since launch it had become home for many of the survivors.

The system was kept in balance through very efficient recycling and reconditioning of materials. However, there was a slow loss of some of elements. Once they reached the orbital location of the third colony, they again used the ship as a capture device to gather the small particles of rock, dust, ice and whatever else was contained in the ring circling the giant orb.

Material capture was planned for the entire time the third colony would take to establish itself. This capture would be processed into usable gases, minerals, and soil. It would be the margin the crew would need to continue its journey.

The materials were gathered and processed in the center section of the Confluence. Here the materials were analyzed, the ice melted, the minerals separated and processed. The crew had studied how to convert various minerals into the finished materials they needed. All the conversion systems were small versions of what previously had been built on the Home Orb.

The crew members collaborated with the survivors on the Home Orb to develop their miniature versions of metal smelters and other production systems. This intense exchange between the Confluence and the Home Orb kept all the survivors connected and engaged.

The continuing exchange served the purpose of getting the crew and colonists educated.

Lamins organized an educational program leading to degrees in a wide variety of fields. It was an idea he had during the transit out to the third colony site. He identified teachers for each level of education. He enrolled each crew member and the Home Orb either as students or teachers. There were only a few people at the very highest levels but many capable teachers in a wide variety of fields. The teachers were spread throughout the crew, the colonists going down to each orb and the survivors at the Home Orb.

Since the survivors at the Home orb were the oldest and most educated, they were usually the instructors at the highest levels. Everyone was encouraged to participate in the field of their choice. The system was made available online to everyone.

Lamins scheduled the classes to start when the Confluence reached the orbit of the third colony. He named it the Solar Academy of Learning. It would issue degrees in every field that was taught.

Nadia and a team created a library to containing the Orbian history. This library became the central focus of the education system. The terra bytes of information in the memory cubes were organized and made available to all.

She hoped that one day the library would house all the material that had been in the Ulm University library.

As the long term became clearer to Nadia and Lamins, they organized the crew into a functioning community. The maintenance and support, work was divided among all the crew. This was based on role, age, the capabilities of the individual and most importantly the desire of the individual.

A common denominator was the work of tending to the plants and the production of food. This was done by all.

But as in any community the largest amount of work was in the maintenance of fundamental support systems. The required work was identified and staffed. None of these systems had been in the design of the rockets as originally launched. Almost every system needed for long term survival needed to be designed and implemented. These had never been envisioned by the individuals launching the rockets.

In the journey out to the fifth orb, Nadia set up a cafeteria led by a "Chef." It featured all the best dishes the Confluence could produce. She remembered her mother's saying about a well-fed soul was a happy soul. The Chefs learned to cook a wide variety of dishes by taking lessons from Lamens's mother.

The crew had a very positive response to this change.

Nadia made sure to share the learning opportunity with each of the surviving colonies.

She also made sure the improvement plans for the Confluence focused on a way to create a pleasant atmosphere.

The rock on Hope was harder than expected and the boring of the vertical tunnel was going slower than planned. The initial contingent had been able to establish temporary quarters. They were rapidly building their above ground facility. Utilizing both the material from the drilling and an abundant supply of above ground boulders, rocks, and finer granules a thick wall structure was built. It became clear this structure was more important than originally thought. The structure would initially house the entire colony. Later when the horizontal living area down in the foot of the vertical shaft was cut out, the colony would move down into the mantle. They would ensure the pressure in the lowest level would be at the norm for their species.

The design of the above ground facility took into account the volume of rock to be brought up from below. It would be added to the structure both internally and externally to provide protection from the tremendous atmospheric pressure. It was similar to the undersea dome in their Home Orb. The lessons learned there were now being utilized. One of the designers of the Home Orb sea structure was in the survivor group on the Home Orb. He reviewed the design and provided key structural tips on making the structure stronger. The shape was in the form of a dome some forty feet thick. The time required to build the structure took much longer than originally planned.

The Confluence remained in a parallel orbit for the entire time the dome was being built.

During this time, the Confluence continued its own transition. The modifications of the Confluence had several side benefits. Nadia came to realize at least one fourth of the survivors would spend their entire life in space. She charged the design team to create a comfortable environment. The gardens incorporated hot pools and areas where to sit and relax. A path for walking and running went around the entire circumference of the Confluence.

A team working with Milan engineered a plant whose sap could be catalyzed into a waterproof, flexible structure of various shapes. Catalysts would activate the chemicals and cause it to coalesce and maintain the shape of the form they were in. This provided a new source of building materials to use in the modification of the Confluence.

The breakthrough gave Nadia hope the Confluence could indeed be a permanent home to the remaining survivors. There were many modifications needed if the ship were to continue to remain in space for a long duration.

By the time, the third colony completed their external structure and was ready to bring the remainder of their population down, the redesign of Confluence and the long-term perspective of those remaining was taking shape.

Lamens and Nadia spent many hours with the Confluence design team in making additional expansion plans. A great amount of additional building material would be required to enable implementing the expansion plans.

Communication with the Home Orb survivors was now a routine and scheduled occurrence. There was a daily condition report from the Orb survivors, each colony and about the Confluence itself. There were scheduled educational classes and there were readings, singing and general personal communication. A small communication team on the Confluence became the primary managers of the system. The time cycle for this communication system continued to be based on the Orbian rotational cycle. The programs used the entire time cycle and then were repeated in a prescheduled way.

Finally, they were ready for the next journey outward.

Nadia wondered about the next colony and the journey out. She had misgivings based on the value of time.

<u>Chapter 16: Home Orb Progress</u>

Raulens, Keren and the others tasked with moving the bodies to their final resting places were emotionally numb. Even with the use of the exoskeletons they were physically exhausted. The number of dead found in Ulm and New Ulm was more than one million. The realization that these beings had survived the initial confluence and lived only to suffocate weighed heavily on the survivors.

The foraging teams discovered several food processing facilities with significant inventories of packaged food. The locations and the quantities were recorded. Food would remain abundant for the foreseeable future.

A team to manage the food supply was established and charged with moving the needed amount to the survival chamber. This team was allocated two suits, two exoskeletons and two flatbed wagons to move the food inventory. This team was later also put in charge of moving other various goods and items needed for the survival chamber.

Another team established pressurized chambers at strategic levels in Ulm and New Ulm. These chambers provided local support to the parties doing work in Ulm and New Ulm. A comprehensive communication system connected all of the chambers.

Key support facilities needed to be organized and put into operation. These included equipment manufacturing and machine shops. Once located each facility was sealed, linked to the communication system, and made self-sufficient.

Those volunteering for work in the various facilities lived at those locations. The arrangement helped distribute the survivors so that they would all have ample room.

There were not enough pressurized suits to allow easy movement to and from the survival chamber. Each location had a minimum of four workers and at least one suit.

The first order of business was the making of oxygen generators. The design had previously been developed for use in the deep-sea domes. The fundamental design was an air collection and pressurization system. These systems worked well. They could not be built fast enough.

Generators to break down various elements found in the mantle and capture the oxygen would be the next version to be developed.

Production of the needed equipment, given the conditions, was at best a slow process, very manual and often had machines now powered by Orbian muscle.

The exoskeleton production facility was one of the big work centers. The team began to turn out one exoskeleton per six work cycles. These additional exoskeletons allowed a greater number of Orbians to participate in the heavy external work.

A new simplified exoskeleton design greatly improved the mobility of the teams in the field.

The need for exoskeletons was second only to the need for more oxygen suits. The spacesuits designed to go out with the rockets worked well in the Orbian atmosphere. However, they were very constraining and made the user seem clumsy. A new simplified version comprised of a tight elastic body glove with what looked like diving goggles and a diver's breathing apparatus was designed. A ceramic oxygen tank was carried on the users back.

The team making these units produced a complete outfit at the rate of five each work cycle. The materials were all readily available and abundant. The goal was to make two of the simplified suits for every individual. These were being produced about five times faster than the exoskeletons. The suites allowed everyone to get out of the survival chamber and move about the exterior.

The ability to go out and about improved the emotional status of the entire survival population. Even with the planned rotation, everyone had the equivalent of tunnel fever.

Milan became the administrator of the survival chamber. She organized the work, got volunteers, and ensured the support for the external workers were in place. Triansa was her second and together they ensured a smooth recovery operation.

Good, organized communication became a primary necessity. Keren salvaged a complete communication center used on the tram system. This system was brought to the survival chamber and set up. Each field team operated on their own frequency. However, every team could quickly be connected with everyone on the system. A radio operator at the center coordinated and supported the field teams. There was one central coordinator for each team. The team members each carried their own communicators and were in constant dialogue with their handlers.

A three-dimensional city map of both Ulm and New Ulm was set up. Green areas indicated the pressurized chambers. The radio operators moved small figures to the location where their team members were operating. This approach proved to be very good at ensuring the safety of the teams. It also provided the field team with special orientation that they often missed as they moved about the various tunnels.

It was full time work keeping track of all the field teams and their specific situation but given the unknown conditions each team would face it was a necessity.

The communication to the Confluence also came to this central communication control center.

The business part of the communication was handled by a dedicated team assigned to communicate with the Confluence.

The online University communications came through the system but was routed to a series of desks with computers salvaged from the public library. The instructors and trainers each had their own broadcast rooms. This allowed the students the necessary access without impeding the normal communication with the Confluence or the other recovery work.

There was never any dead airtime. The differences in time of the various students meant that the teachers operated around the clock and there was a minimum of two teachers for each subject.

The living standards in the survival chamber improved dramatically as the materials from the apartments in Ulm were brought back. Each family or group wanting to live together received the materials to set up a private apartment.

Survival was slowly becoming easier. The quantity of materials available for salvage would sustain the survivors for their entire lives.

Everyone knew the materials on which they were living had been paid for with the lives of their brethren Orbians. There was a Confluence ceremony every quarter period to commemorate those who had died.

Each team also had an individual responsible for recording what was found and where it was located. This was carefully entered into a database that one of the computer programmers had established. Most materials were left where they were found. Food resources were the first to be recorded. Then all the raw materials for construction were catalogued.

The libraries of information and their condition were reviewed and improved by a librarian team.

The red dots indicating the deceased always disturbed Milan. She had taken on the ongoing responsibility for taking the personal information of the bodies found by the salvage teams. A team to move the bodies to the morgue went out once every five cycles. Usually, they would move several thousand bodies. It would take the survivors their lifetime to find all the bodies.

Many levels of Ulm had been purged by the waters at Confluence. Many levels of Ulm seemed untouched. Many levels of Ulm would never be re-opened. The sealed floors were designated on the city map and a burial ceremony was conducted for those interred within.

The city's population had been three hundred million. There were roughly fifteen hundred survivors. Sealing the various areas was their only way of handling a situation beyond their capabilities and resources.

The initial goal for the survivors was to ensure their food and air supply. Managing the dead became their second task. In took three cycles to reach the point where the areas of Ulm and New Ulm being utilized by the survivors were free of the dead.

The majority of both cities were left unexplored. There were just not enough survivors to continue the burial work. Any time a new part of the city was entered to recover some needed resource, more dead were found.

It left all of them with an emotional scar that was repeatedly reopened and then needed re-healing.

I am not sure how many times I am capable of recovering and stepping back from the edge of insanity," Raulens confided to both Milan and Keren one evening after and especially grueling day of moving several thousand dead bodies.

"There really is no stepping back. I think we will just become very different people than we would have been in our other world before the Confluence," Keren responded.

"Yes, I believe we are different, but I believe we are stronger. We must be if we are to survive," Milan added.

The study of the maps of each city showed the main tunnels had been purged by the waters flowing through during the Confluence. Secondary tunnels were less damaged, and the really remote ones were untouched. The industrial sectors had survived damage better than the lighter constructed residential areas. Ulm was more intact than New Ulm.

The difference appeared to be the more modern and efficient boring technique used in the construction of New Ulm. The newer design created a better-connected tunnel system. The waters surging through during the Confluence found less resistance and penetrated New Ulm almost totally. The design had never considered the possibility of the flow of supersonic water going through.

Finally, almost three cycles after the Confluence, the survivors began expanding their living area. One contingent was locating itself in Ulm at the University. They established themselves in the University Student Center facility.

Raulens and Milan moved to this new location. Many of Raulens friends were professors at the University. Most chose to move with him back to Ulm.

Plans for this new location included a new communication center. Living quarters were located adjacent to the cafeteria area. Gardens were established in several of the halls connecting the student center with specific colleges. The University Library was next door to the Student Center. This had been a key reason for the choice of the student center as the living quarters. The initial evaluation of the area indicated the library and many of the surrounding colleges would be able to be sealed and pressurized to create a very large living space for the seven hundred planning to move back.

The move to these new locations invigorated every Orbian.

The Planetarium would never rise on its elevator system again. The containment lid was extremely heavy and the energy to activate the drive motors might never be available. The containment had protected all the equipment in the Planetarium. It would eventually be sealed and pressurized. Perhaps its computers could eventually be reenergized.

If at all possible, Raulens wanted to get all the records from the planetarium computers. He asked a team of computer experts to come up with a way to extract all the information.

The choice of where to live was left up to each individual.

Keren chose to establish himself at the chambers of the Ulm Orb Council.

The interconnections between various chambers and the security gates facilitated dividing the area into zones. The zone with the cafeteria and the long connections to the meeting chambers were sealed. Living quarters and gardens were built in converted offices and meeting rooms. The system in the security office was reactivated and needed little modification to serve as the communication center.

Several of Kerens friends moved back to this location. One of these friends had become his partner. Mislan was sister to one of the young boys in Nadia's crew. Mislan had been in the group discovered alive by Raulens in his first excursion to Ulm.

Learning of this romantic situation was one of the few bright moments Milan had experienced since the Confluence.

"It lifts one of the weights from my heart," Milan told Raulens when she learned of the pairing.

"Yours and mine as well," Raulens replied as he gave Milan a hug.

He suggested that they hold a family celebration to recognize both of their cubs having found their mates.

In all roughly three hundred moved to the Council Location that Keren had established.

The rest stayed in the survival chamber. The chamber was remodeled to provide a better environment. Exercise facilities, a formal cafeteria, and an entertainment facility were all added. The survival chamber changed its appearance dramatically.

The area outside leading to the original rail line was cleared and the containment area expanded. This made the survival area one of the most spacious of the living facilities.

At the end of the first full Orb cycle after the establishment of the three groups, Raulens' group invited the other two to the first Ulm Survivors Celebration. The Student Union cafeteria was large enough to seat everyone. The main dishes of squashes and melons were provided by Raulens' group. The visiting groups were asked to bring enough salads and desserts to feed everyone else. This event was a major turning point for the survivor groups.

They had now survived four cycles.

Nadia had heard of the upcoming celebration and had composed a song and new melody. She and several of the crew members who had formed a singing group recorded the song.

This song was a broadcast surprise from the crew of the Confluence.

<u>Chapter 17: Inward or Outward</u>

The consideration of the next leg of the outward colonization manifested itself as an assault of time. The distances were so great and the speed of the Confluence a snail's pace in contrast to mind numbing distance. The next leg out would take three cycles. If there was a habitable orb the Confluence would need to spend at least two cycles establishing another colony.

The astronomers identified three potential orbs circling the next major orb. They found a similar number circling the final large orb. All of these potential sites were only one half to one third the size of the orbs chosen for the current colonies.

Nadia and Lamins conferred with Raulens and a group on the Home Orb. The wisdom of continuing the journey outward was questioned. The dramatically smaller size of the sites was the key tipping factor.

"What I have seen and what I have felt in the establishment of the first colonies diminishes my will to go out and risk that these smaller satellites will be adequate. It seems pointless," Nadia spoke her mind and knew that the Confluence was not going any farther out.

She was not going to risk her remaining crew members or risk not being in the right place when one of the colonies need some support.

After considering the risks and the problems of making these smaller orbs functional everyone reached the same conclusion and supported the decision of discontinuing the outward journey.

Nadia was certain the decision was the correct one to make.

"I am already concerned with the colonies we have established. Their environments already stretch our capabilities. These sites even farther out are less promising and cost us dearly in the time to go and come back," Nadia commented to the online team.

The news from the first two colonies was mixed. Both were making slow progress. The cold had cost the lives of several of their number. The gardens were continuing to produce and the soil on both colonies was rich in nutrients.

Raulens and his team, back on the Home Orb, were providing guidance on how the colonists could improve the production of electrical energy.

The colony on Hope had an abundance of energy. Their challenge was to establish their living environment deep within the mantle. Their greatest threat came from the very abundance of energy available to them. The entire orb was a potential chemical bomb.

Nadia felt relieved to be going back to the first two colonies.

By the time of the decision to not go any farther out, the Confluence had been out in space for ten Orbian cycles. This was almost one third of the normal life span for an Orbian. The three colonies were slowly establishing themselves. The survivors on the Home Orb had made considerable progress and were now well established.

A key concern to Nadia was the lack of any births. Some critical factor was preventing even the desired pregnancy.

She thought of her situation. She and Lamins were living as partners. In the past getting pregnant was a conscious decision of the female.

This was not true in the current environment.

If it were possible, she would lead by example. She was nearing the end of her normal childbearing years.

"We need to find out what the cause is in our lack of giving birth to the next generation. I am putting together a study team to determine what it may be," Nadia announced during one of the communications meetings with the Home Orb.

After reviewing the history cubes Nadia's research team discovered the species protected itself from the radiation surges on their Home Orb by inhibiting the cycle of pregnancy. The current radiation exposure was bearable for them to function normally, but the level of their radiation exposure remained high.

This evidently was affecting all of them.

Nadia was silent upon learning of this situation.

There was no place to hide.

There was no magnetic field to shield any of the colonies.

There would be no births.

She concluded that in reality they had all died at the moment of the Confluence.

They inadvertently named their ship after the instrument of their death.

She privately consulted with Milan and Raulens. They agreed with the research done on the Confluence. The magnetic field of the Home Orb had been weakened even farther by the interaction with the black void. A similar conclusion was reached by the Home Orb team.

It appeared the radiation was preventing births, but it seemed to be extending the life spans of the older Confluence population. There was a steady decay of the surviving population. Accidents claimed about twenty percent. Age was beginning to claim the older leaders. Nadia seemed to be the exception. She was aging gracefully. She was now twenty-one cycles in age.

The average life expectancy on her Home Orb was thirty-five.

Some of the older Orb survivors the had succumbed to old age. Milan and Raulens were now each thirty-six cycles of age. They were both surprised they had lasted this long.

The Confluence was a full cycle away on its return to the first two colonies when the depressing news came from the Milan colony. Their thermal gradient energy source was not delivering enough energy to fight off the piercing cold. The colony was losing ground. They did not know how much longer they would survive. The gardens were not producing enough food. They needed help.

The Confluence was a half an orb cycle away. They had no way to provide any direct help.

The fear of such a thing had been one of the concerns that Nadia had expressed early in the colonization process.

The expert resources on the Home Orb reviewed the design of the energy generation system. They came up with several modifications leading to a thirty percent energy generation improvement. The modifications were immediately executed. There was an immediate improvement. This increase allowed the gardens to get back into full production. The colony was still short on energy, but they would survive until the Confluence was back in orbit to provide direct aid.

The Milan Colony's rescue by the Home Orb group caused that colony to declare a Home Orb Celebration day

A day did not pass when Nadia did not suffer some period of depression. Each time she thought of the moment of Confluence she recoiled at the memory. She had no control over the tears she shed.

The news from Milan took her in a new direction. She realized the survivors on the ship, down on the colonies and back on the Home Orb all were on a much slower journey into the same oblivion.

Nadia chartered a group to organize and store all of the history of their species. These were organized on memory crystals each capable of holding the entire history of their species.

Nadia planned one more cycle for the Confluence. She would return to their Home Orb. Anyone wanting to return to the Home Orb and descent to the surface could do so.

She estimated the trip back would take three cycles. The Confluence would spend a full cycle with the Home Orb. When it came around in the alignment, they would return to Raulens to spend a cycle with them. Then they would proceed outward at least once more to Hope. This would take another six cycles. In all the Confluence designed to make the journey to the third orb and be out in space the short period of a half a cycle was already out for almost twelve cycles.

The Confluence would outlast its crew. There were now only nine hundred in the crew and each of the three colonies had roughly the same number. The rate of decline if it remained linear indicated the end of the Orbian population would happen out about twenty cycles in the future.

Nadia did not yet know what the minimum thresh hold would be for each of the colonies or for those on the Home Orb. She figured the Confluence minimum crew size was around ten. This meant it would be able to function with only a few remaining crew. She knew the number required to maintain any of the three colonies would be higher. This meant the colonies would cease existence first. The last survivors would most likely be on the Home Orb.

One of the tasks was to find a place where the Confluence could be put to rest. A stable orbit around one of the orbs or a resting place on one of the many smaller moons were a few of the options she and Lamins discussed. They came to the conclusion they would seek a place close to the colony at Raulens. This location allowed the Confluence to support two colonies as long as possible.

Hope continued to make progress in the development of their living quarters. They had reached their planned vertical depth and were beginning to build their final living areas. The dome structure had been evacuated to the pressure they could work in without the need for the low-pressure vessels.

This made all the work easier and quicker. The Hope colony was the most advanced, stable, and successful. They were in the best shape of all the colonies.

The colony on Raulens was not as stable as Hope and they were working on stabilizing their living areas. They were literally floating in a sea of ice. They were also sinking at the measurable rate of about an inch each cycle. This meant either periodically lifting the colony or in about a thousand Orbian cycles they would reach the bottom.

The sinking was a secondary concern.

The Confluence was now capable of replenishing the Raulens colony with about a cycle worth of additional food supply. This was gratefully accepted by the colony. They continued to generate enough energy and their gardens were still performing well but they welcomed having the extra insurance.

Next the Confluence established an orbit as close to Milan as possible. A large quantity of food was sent down to ensure any additional problems with the gardens could be managed. Then the piping required to install two more temperature gradient wells was sent down.

The Confluence factory had developed an extruding technique to produce a plastic like piping. This would serve as the casing for the energy wells. The heat gradient piping was coiled internal to the large casing. Each new well would be able to produce four times the energy produced by the original two wells.

This would provide enough energy to comfortably heat the living quarters. For the first time the settlers on Milan would experience enough warmth to be comfortable.

All the colonies were doing well. The ability to communicate and help each other made a huge difference in the progress of each colony. It also eased the stress each felt about their situation. Hearing about the problems each faced helped the individuals in the colonies to regenerate their enthusiasm and their mental energy.

Though the attitude of the crew and the colonists seemed upbeat, it did not escape Nadia that no new births had occurred. This was rare for their species. She inquired about this with the first two colonies and the survivors on the Home Orb. All reported no births, and none were expected. This was unprecedented.

Raulens knew he was now really old. He had been twenty-seven at the time of Confluence. Now twelve cycles later he was beyond the normal life expectancy. He was not yet ready to give in. Milan was this exact age, and she too was not ready. The two supported each other and were each other's energy.

"I never thought to be this old. And of course, I never could have imagined what our future would be like. Now I just want to survive to know that our species will survive," Raulens commented to Milan.

"I never thought you would be so old either. How did I ever get tangled up with some old Orbian," Milan joked back.

Neither of them was working in their original field of expertise. They were working hard at trying to overcome the lack to births. This meant the study of their anatomy and the life generation cycle of their species.

Surprisingly, little work had been done in this field. Birthing had never been a point of concern. There was little documentation on the gestation cycle.

They quietly did autopsies on some of the dead females to get a better understanding of the physical design of the female reproductive system.

They slowly developed an understanding of how the reproductive system worked. There seemed to be two controlling factors.

One was the mental signal to the body to become pregnant.

The other was a non-controllable internal signal from the brain or some organ indicating it was safe to get pregnant.

Discussions with Nadia and Keren's partner confirmed both were mentally trying to make it happen.

It was Nadia who almost accidentally came up with the solution. During the remodeling of the Confluence and the addition of more radiation shielding, she suggested additional radiation shielding for the female desiring to get pregnant.

Lamins surprised her two days later with an outfit made of gold. He also tripled the radiation shielding in the areas Nadia spent most of her time.

Within ten work cycles Nadia was pregnant.

This news was quickly shared with everyone.

The news was joyously received by Milan and Raulens. For them it was a miracle that their beloved daughter would be the first to expand the population. And it gave them a new purpose. They wanted to see their next generation.

A large number of pregnancies followed.

On the Home Orb the surplus food ensured sustenance would not be an issue.

Generating the required oxygen for the additional population would be the challenge. Raulens asked a few scientists to determine the population limit they needed to consider for each of the population groups. Their findings were mixed.

Tripling the population of the Home Orb was the current limit based on the amount of oxygen they could generate.

The populations on Milan could double if space and food were available. Energy would be the limit for them.

On Raulens the limit was only space and food.

Hope was the colony with no current limits as long as food production was expanded. Overall, this was positive.

The decline Nadia originally projected to a limit of twenty-three years for the race was now leveled.

They could maintain their current levels, but growth of the population was a shadow of their previous population.

Nadia's next song gave thanks to her mate who had given her a golden dress, to her brother who had the vision to surreptitiously place her mate where she would not miss seeing him. She finished the song by described the future growth of the Orbian population.

Chapter 18: Return to the Home Orb

The Confluence loaded up on raw materials as they went around the giant Orb while they accompanied the Raulens colony. The Confluence crew had improved their ability to move into a stream of material at matching speeds and then vacuum in the materials that surrounded them.

They were collecting materials to replenish the Confluence's stock of minerals, water, critical gases. The collection was random in the sense they could only collect the materials available in the orbiting debris and they could not be selective. However, all the materials were useful, so it did not matter. Their main goal was to maximize what they could capture.

During this cycle Lamins and a design team developed a plan to increase the radiation shielding of the Confluence. Several of the crew proposed a relatively straightforward way to construct the thicker shielding. A layer of ceramic tiles would be applied to the exterior of the ship. Radiation protection would be a matter of the material the tiles were made of and of adjusting the thickness of the exterior coverage. They could pluck the material from space and add to the shielding.

The effect of the additional mass would be minimal. It would only take a small additional supplement of fuel to maintain the Confluence's rotation.

Several of the gardeners in communication with Milan back on the Home Orb developed a plant whose sap mixed with a few other chemicals would create a very strong flexible membrane. This membrane along with some glue-like sap from another plant simplified the construction of the exterior radiation wall.

The ceramic bricks were formed from finely ground material packed into a slightly curved form. The powder was heavily compressed and removed from the form then sent through an oven and heated for several clicks. After a short cooling period the bricks were ready to be applied to the exterior.

The balance of the rotating ship needed to be maintained. When a sufficient number of bricks were ready, the number was divided in half. Half of the bricks were added on one side of the wheel and the other half was added across from them on the opposite side of the ship. Two teams went on the outside and applied the small batch of bricks. Every work cycle two hundred bricks were positioned and locked in place by using the membrane. The original two T sections were shielded first. The ease and the success caused the design teams to expand their thinking.

As fast as the material was collected, it was processed and made into ceramic bricks, and applied to the exterior of the Confluence. The brick making was slightly faster than the application of brick on the exterior. Soon the inventory of extra brick was being stored in the central section of the ship.

The center section and the first two T sections were completed while still in orbit with the Raulens colony. The captured material was enough to provide full radiation coverage.

Additional full radiation shielding would be applied as the Confluence made its journey to the Home Orb.

Nadia and the leadership team realized the Confluence could be expanded in the same manner as the shielding was being done. Lamins and his team designed additional sections to be built from the center to each of the wheel sections.

A flexible membrane in the form of a tube was produced in the diameter of the existing T section. Special interlocking ceramic bricks were designed for this purpose. The new sections were simple to build. The construction was similar to laying a normal brick wall. The snap together design, and the membrane acted to hold the bricks in place. A special adhesive sap was used to seal the joints between the bricks. The internal floors added the linear structural integrity required to keep the tubes rigid.

Eight construction teams were commissioned. Eight ceramic firing ovens were set up in addition to the ones making the radiation bricks for the exterior of the ship.

The Confluence was arriving to the debris that populated where a fifth Orb should have been.

"We are coming to where there is even more material available. We will make a concerted effort to get all the materials needed to completely recompose the original design of the Confluence and the additional material to make ever better radiation shielding," Lamins informed his design team.

Lamins planned a slow journey through this area. The Confluence entered and angled slowly through in the same direction the particles of the field were traveling. Their course was plotted to bring them out the other side at the closest as possible to the position of their Home Orb. They would remain in the field almost a third of an orb cycle.

The teams gathered materials continuously. They split the cycle into three and adjusted their staffing to keep the entire process flowing. The entire process from debris capture to brick placement flowed in a continuous stream.

Lamins marveled at the smoothness and coordination of the process. This teamwork was what had made the Orbians the dominant species on their Orb.

"I am seeing a display of productivity that I can only marvel at and brag about," Lamins reported at one of the communication meetings with the Home Orb.

Construction was almost complete when the time to leave the field arrived. Lamins and the captains decided to stay in the field for an additional seven work cycles. This would allow all construction and shielding to be completed. It was an easy decision since there was no specific action required on their arrival to the Home Orb. In fact, the crew was a little uneasy about their return. They were not sure what they could do once in orbit around the Home Orb.

The material collected was analyzed and separated based on composition. Oxygen rich material was processed, and the oxygen was stored in liquid form in pressurized tanks.

Materials with heavy metals were processed to a purer form.

Sands were collected to provide glazing for the bricks and other objects being produced.

The expansion of the gardens was supported with soil rich in nutrients. All of this new material was stored in the outer layers of the Confluence. The newly built sections with much better shielding would be used by the crew for work areas.

The rough internal construction of the new T sections was almost complete by the time the Confluence went into orbit around the Home Orb.

The interior finish work on the new T sections and expansion of gardens and modification of living space would continue during the time the Confluence orbited. Additional recreation space was also planned and would be constructed in the near future.

"This is the best attitude and energy that I have seen in the crew," Nadia complimented Lamins on his reconstitution of the Confluence.

The additional shielding cut the internal radiation to the same level as originally experienced on the Home Orb. It was not the breakthrough shielding hoped for, but it provided the margin of safety to make the journey home and back out feasible.

As they arrived back to the origin of their journey, Lamins and Nadia reviewed the Confluence survivor's accomplishments.

The survivors had constructed the Confluence as they left their cherished but demolished Home Orb.

The survivors had gone out into the orbital system and established three successful colonies around two giant Orbs.

They had expanded the Confluence.

They had survived in space for more than twelve cycles.

Their newly established production and manufacturing capability was extensive.

And most important, they had solved the problem of perpetuating their species.

The positive change in the crew was obvious to Nadia.

There was now an upbeat feeling and conversation seemed easier.

Relaxation in the paths and gardens was now occurring.

There was hope in the air.

Nadia and two other females were pregnant and would give birth as they journeyed around the sun with their Home Orb.

Nadia was at peace.

Her race would not flourish as it might have at one time but in a short time it had achieved a rapid expansion throughout the orbital system.

Now she would pass on her family line at least into the foreseeable future. She was as close to home as she could be for this event.

The Home Orb appeared the same as when Nadia left it twelve cycles ago. She could not see much change on the surface. She knew from the reports Keren, Milan or Raulens sent of the progress and rebuilding occurring.

The population of the home colony was only two thousand strong. It was impossible for this number to restart the Ulm complex. They could only mine its resources.

Resources for this colony were not an issue.

The ability to utilize and maintain the complex structure of Ulm was the issue.

The population on the Home Orb could reach as high as ten thousand before sustainability issues associated with oxygen generation were reached.

Raulens and Milan were now forty-six cycles of age. This made them the oldest among all the survivors and ancient by any measure of age. They were well beyond the average life expectancy of thirty-six. They joked they were good for another thirty-six. Seeing their first grandchild was now their goal.

Raulens had a surprise for the Confluence. He had devised a way for a cable connection from the Confluence to the surface to be achieved. The only challenge was to create a cable of enough length and strength and a way to send it down to the surface. This connection would allow travel up and down to be powered by a simple motor that would ride the cable. Materials and personnel could then travel up and down the cable.

This news sent excitement through the entire Confluence crew.

Nadia was exuberant. Perhaps she would be able to physically hug her family one more time.

Determining how to make the material for the cable and then making enough cable became the primary point of discussion.

It at first seemed unachievable.

Milan had been working on this problem. The same plant so efficient at providing the ingredients for the membrane currently being utilized to hold the bricks on the outside of the Confluence could be used to create a flexible and elastic fiber with the strength required to fabricate the cable.

This possibility caused Nadia and her leadership team to reassess their goals for the visit.

Originally Nadia planned the visit as a goodbye to those she knew.

Now a new opportunity presented itself. The goal became the development and execution of an elevator from the Confluence to the surface. This would allow the transfer of personnel and resources in both directions.

The only issue was the ability to grow the amount of material needed.

Once again Raulens provided a solution.

The Confluence would only need to provide the fiber for a very thin line with enough strength to pull a line double its size back up to the Confluence.

The Home Orb would grow and produce the actual elevator cable and the components to make up the entire system. A series of ever thicker cables would be sent up to the confluence until finally the actual elevator cable system would be pulled into place. After this first use the elevator system could be pulled up by the Confluence for its future use.

The length of this thin cable was astounding to think about. If a low synchronous orbit were maintained. The total length was two hundred, sixty-five thousand clicks and it would need to be stored in a fashion allowing a continuous feed down to the surface of the Orb.

"I am asking the crew for all ideas on how we can create and then handle this unprecedented length of cable," Nadia made her public request of the entire team.

The answer the crew came up with was to make the Confluence into a giant cable reel.

This idea came from one of the young females that told her peers about how her grandmother had these reels of thread that seemed to go on forever.

The cable could be wrapped around the outside of the center module. The Confluences natural rotation would be used to reel and un-reel the cable. The Confluence end of the cable would attach to the center module on the end. The outer level of this module was converted to become the receiving area.

The elevator container that traveled up the cable would be built so its outside diameter was just slightly less that the inside diameter of Confluences central module. This elevator module would be built by the Home Orb team. The Confluence crew would build the receiving station and the entrance connections. The elevator module would crawl up the elevator cable and be pulled into the receiving area.

"Thank heavens for grandmothers," Nadia announced when the concept had been turned into actual construction plans.

Once the cable was to be reeled in, it would be guided to a catch on the outer lip of the central cylinder. The large elevator cable would then be guided to wrap around the outside of the central cylinder. A counterweight on the other end of the central cylinder would move inward or outward along the cylinder to act as counterweight needed to keep the Confluence in balance.

Providing the power for this system was another challenge. The confluence had been launched with solid fueled rocket engines. Now they needed liquid fueled engines to create the force to pull the cable up. The few engines they had were used to maintain their current one gravity equivalent rotating velocity.

The materials to build the engines were available and the Confluence's manufacturing capability had increase sufficiently and could produce these needed engines.

The fuel for them was a more precious resource. The estimate of the fuel needed was at the limit of their resources. The balance of what the gardens were growing was adjusted to increase the capability for additional fuel generation.

It was very lucky they had stored up on extra materials when they went through the debris orbit. All of the material would now be utilized to meet the challenges of this new goal.

Nadia thought about the gardens. Without them, there would be no survivors except on the Home Orb. She would ask Milan for all additional new plants developed on the Home Orb and any other plants missed for her first gardens.

"I am so pleased to be able to think about expanding our gardens and about getting new ones. I wonder, are there any quizl survivors?" Nadia commented on one of her conversations with Milan.

"Yes, I took a family into the survival chamber with me. I have been out in the canyons and have found about twenty more. I have been feeding all of them. Either they are reproducing faster than I remember that they are capable of, or they have sent out the message that there is food at my door," Milan replied.

There was enough material on the confluence to create the counterweight required if two of the just completed new T sections were sacrificed. This counterweight would be built in four sections and kept to the center of the Confluence until the cable to the surface was being pulled up. The material was stored. It would need to be quickly assembled and put into position on the cable connection had been achieved.

The gardens and growing the super fiber producing plant became the key focus on the Confluence. Everyone was constantly trying to help. The cable was a multi-fiber, multi-dimension, zigzag weave. It would only be a digit in thickness. Its quality and consistency needed to be flawless. The weave was necessary to allow it to stretch elastically and give.

The challenge of holding the Confluence in a steady, synchronous orbit required to maintain an elevator to the surface was a worry that Nadia and Lamens talked about every cycle.

"Our crew will need to practice, practice, practice and then practice some more," Lamens mumbled to himself.

Ron Mueller

Chapter 19: Journey to the Third Orb

Conversations with Raulens led Nadia to decide on an exploratory journey to the Third Orb. This was a trip Nadia wished to make. It would give her the opportunity to determine if a colony were an option for the Third Orb. It would also answer many of the questions she and Raulens both had about the life on the Orb. The decision was sealed when Lamins and Keren pointed out that it would add to their search for a future home so critical for the survival of their race.

The journey to the Third Orb was agreed to by the Confluence leadership team. This time the shielding was sufficient for the crew to function. Super shielded sections in the newer section of the Confluence offered the recovery areas needed for crew health to remain high.

The journey in would take about one-half cycle of the Home Orb. The round trip was almost exactly the time needed to produce the thin pull cable. The crew left their Home Orb in an energized state and excited about taking the journey to the Blue Jewel. This was the nickname they had given the Third Orb. This time their journey was one filled with hope versus despair.

Raulens requested pictures. He also wanted Nadia to use her telescopes to closely examine the land and sea for life.

"Look for any sign of intelligent beings. They may be more primitive than we and only have caves or other structures to live in," Raulens sent his message as the Confluence left the Home Orb.

"By all means Milan, you must keep me alive until we see our grandchild and I get to see the surprises the Blue Jewel holds," Raulens commented.

Nadia would give birth on her way to the third Orb. She was excited by the occurrence. Given her age, this would most likely be her only child.

Milan was as excited as she. Milan suggested the name given the third colony, Hope, as the name for this child. This would make all the colonies members of the same family. Lamins was in agreement with this idea.

Seeing Nadia happy for the first time in almost twelve cycles made Lamins personally content and happy as well.

"I have been blessed to live with the woman of my dreams. And now we will have an offspring," I am as happy as I could be in any environment.

As the time for giving birth neared, Nadia passed her work out to the various leaders on the leadership team. She spent her time examining the Blue Orb. Each day she would take a series of pictures and post them for everyone to see. She planned a day-by-day mural to run the length of the internal walking path. Everyone made it a point to examine the ever-growing world ahead of them.

A picture of the newborn was posted on the morning of its birth. She was named Hope. It was also the first day the telescope could clearly see a huge continent on the Blue Orb.

Hope came into the world with a cheerful cry. She had her mother's eyes and her father's smile. Hope was happy to see and be held by all the crew.

Within days she had been cuddled and held by every crew member.

The second pregnant crew member gave birth to a male only a few days later. She named him Hedris after her father. His picture went on the wall along with an even clearer picture of the huge green continent surrounded by water.

Young Orbians were very energetic and almost immediately mobile and curious. Nadia recruited several young female crew members to help her keep up with Hope. Hope was fond of following her mother but when Nadia turned her attention to the telescope or to some other order of business, Hope would always begin to investigate and get into areas she should stay out of. The task of the helpers was to keep Hope from hurting herself or damaging some item in the room.

Nadia used the occasion to readjust the leadership responsibilities. She promoted one of the Captains to be the permanent Confluence Captain. Neihen was the captain originally volunteering to lead the colony to go down to Keren. He had taken it hard when Keren was deemed too risky. He, however, used his energy to help train the team now on the Hope colony. He was a key team member on the team making the breakthrough on building the radiation shielding.

"I have asked Neihen to act as the captain of the Confluence. My deep confidence and respect for his capabilities makes him a natural selection. His contributions to the colonization efforts and to the rebuilding of the Confluence are recognized by all. He has graciously accepted. Please congratulate him when your get the opportunity," Nadia announced to the Confluence crew and then sent out the message the rest of the survivors.

Lamins made a similar move and promoted two additional crew members to be chief navigators. He too wanted to spend more time with his expanded family.

Additionally, the propulsion and steering of the Confluence was being refined to allow more control of position and speed. This meant there would be the need for additional staffing and practice. This change was taking place on the way to the Blue Orb. The goal was to allow the expanded team time to practice navigation, steering and then controlling the Confluence in orbit around the Blue Orb. They would have twenty work cycles to practice holding the Confluence in synchronous orbit above the massive continent on the Blue Orb.

New thrust rockets were being fabricated and mounting locations being prepared. The Confluence continued its evolution. There was never an idle moment. It was around the cycle continuous work.

Nadia commissioned a special team to study the feasibility of building a second ship when they next crossed the debris belt on the way back to the colonies. She picked most of the team who had designed and built the expansion of the Confluence. She was personally convinced life on a structure such as the Confluence was preferable to the life on any of the current colonies. This included those remaining on the Home Orb. She discussed this with Lamins but had not yet raised the topic with Raulens.

"I want to understand the feasibility of doubling or tripling our space faring capacity. We also need to understand if we can maintain our ships for thousands of Orbian cycles or longer," Nadia shared with Lamens.

She would make this a primary discussion topic when the concept of the cable elevator up to the Confluence became a reality.

"First, let's see if we can really get a sky elevator up and working," Nadia thought to herself.

Nadia turned her full attention to the Blue Orb. She set up a work team of a dozen to help her observe and catalogue what they might find. Almost immediately she could tell it was a vibrant Orb. There were active volcanoes, and the atmosphere was substantial. Water vapor swirled around the land mass.

The moon of this Orb was very large. It was a world of its own. It was more hospitable then the orbs chosen for colonization. The high radiation so close to the Grand Orb was the key factor keeping it from consideration. Perhaps by drilling deep down into the mantle of this moon colonization would be feasible. However, establishing another colony was not the purpose of this journey. Perhaps they would return in the future.

As the Confluence passed the moon and made its approach to an orbit around the Blue Jewel, Nadia examined the large single continent. She and her team commissioned a new larger telescope. It was five times larger and more powerful than the one she originally brought up with her. The lens was made from the materials scavenged from the debris belt. The finest and clearest sands were melted and molded to form a sixty-digit diameter lens. The telescope and its lens were built in the vacuum and weightlessness of one of the center workshops. The quality and precision of the series of lenses and reflecting surfaces was the best Nadia had ever seen. She shared this with Raulens, who had made the last major lens improvement.

She was visibly affected when she aimed it at the surface and was able to see the movement of the huge undulating plants. She wordlessly pulled Lamins to the eye piece to look for himself. She took pictures almost continuously.

The plant life was overwhelming in its size, richness, and variety. The gravity was two and a half times greater, but the plant life was gigantic by any measure. She spotted something moving through the air and realized giant creatures were moving through what she had presumed was just air.

She wondered how they were able to achieve such a capability.

She followed these over the ocean and was amazed to see the shadow of an even larger creature in the water.

What an Orb!

Its creatures were gigantic by any measure.

Nadia could not take herself away from the telescope.

Lamens had to physically pull her away.

The crew trying to hold a synchronous orbit was having some problems. Their calculations seemed to be in error. The Confluence first drifted one way along the continent and then it drifted in the other direction.

This was great practice for the navigators, and it actually helped Nadia in her study of the life she was finding.

The new larger telescope provided an almost life like view.

Nadia glided with the monsters in the sky. She was fascinated by this capability and could not get enough of it.

On land much smaller animals ran in large groups. There was such a variety she was constantly finding a new species. There seemed to be two major kinds of land animals. One was plant eating and the other ate the plant eaters.

She imagined that a similar, but much smaller scale situation occurred early in the Home Orbs history.

She was sure her species would have been the eaters of the plant eaters.

There did not seem to be intelligence as known to the Orbians. It was clear the creatures she was observing had a high level of intelligence. They lived together in large groups. Nadia noted an area she thought of as a safe area for the young.

The herd wandered around the outside of this area, and a few seemed to be guarding the young. These animals looked ferocious and vicious.

Their need to protect themselves from some other group of animals gave Nadia pause. How would the Orbians, now a gentle species fare? It was clear these animals possessed a strong skeletal structure. Their basic composition was similar to the Orbian frame but ten times larger and stronger.

Nadia was also intrigued by the huge creatures in the waters of the ocean surrounding the single huge continent. They were almost the length of one of the Confluence's T sections. Nothing of this size ever existed on the Home Orb. Her species was the largest to have ever populated the Orb and had become the dominant ones.

What she saw below was a world in jubilant, flourishing turmoil. It was enjoying a wide variety of life. The plant and animal life were so extensive the best Nadia could do was to take pictures and put them in a catalogue for later study.

She filled crystal matrix after crystal matrix with the images she captured. This material would take a lifetime or two to analyze. Nadia pictured Raulens studying them for the rest of his days.

Her team worked around the clock taking and cataloguing pictures. They created a giant map of the continent. A grid overlay provided a way for the location of the various plants and animals to be documented. The volumes of material generated in their twenty-four-work cycle stay, filled almost one of the T sections.

The team responsible for keeping the Confluence in synchronous orbit sharpened both their mathematical calculation and the ability of the crew to keep the Confluence in synchronous orbit. This was a crucial capability they would need to enable the use of an elevator lift to the surface of their Home Orb.

The work on constructing the reel system to hold the final cable was proceeding on schedule.

The weaving of the pull line was also proceeding according to plan.

The deconstruction of two T sections and the construction of the counterweight was the work taking the most effort. Nadia wished there as another way to get the necessary material for the counterweight.

She would make sure to pick up the maximum amount of material the Confluence would hold when they went back through the debris field.

Before departure from the Blue Jewel, Nadia consulted with Raulens, Milan, Keren, and Lamins about leaving a history crystal of the Orbian's visit to the third Orb. This would give whatever intelligence developed on the Blue Jewel an indication other intelligences existed.

Everyone was immediately supportive.

Where and how to leave such an item seemed to be the only question. Nadia chose to put the history crystal inside a thick heavy ceramic globe. She in a small ceremony, sent it toward the center of the huge land mass.

She hoped it would survive and be a link with some future intelligence.

It was hard to leave such rich source of knowledge and the site of such vibrant life. Her Home Orb had been destroyed but this Blue Jewel seemed to be flourishing beyond all imagination.

The Confluence slowly made its way out to the huge moon. They would use it to gain the speed they desired for their return trip to their Home Orb. Nadia watched the Moon grow in size on the approach. It was airless and lifeless. It had experienced countless meteor impacts. It was clear that this region also received its share of bombardment from the materials out in space.

"You have my wish for your long-term survival. May the darkness and death of the Confluence never affect your beauty," Nadia thought to herself as she looked into her scope at the receding image of the Blue Jewel.

She marveled at the fact that she had made it to the Third Orb in her lifetime. She also spent some time writing a song to the Blue Jewel of the Grand Orb.

Chapter 20: Up from the Home Orb

The crew of the Confluence was a skilled crew as they guided the Confluence toward the Blue Orb. The crew leaving the Blue Orb had become skilled masters in the roles each played. Their increased skill was easily noticed.

All the members of the Confluence crew demonstrated a revitalized level of energy.

"This journey to the Blue Jewel and our work on establishing a space elevator has totally changed the attitude and atmosphere on the Confluence. For the first time since the beginning, I too have new hope," Nadia shared with Lamens.

"Yes, all of us, even our colonists, have a new sense of hope. There have been and continue to be more births. Even your songs and music are one of new hope," Lamens quietly replied.

The three colonies were holding their own. However, only the colony on Hope was making significant progress. The other two colonies were holding and surviving but it was a very difficult struggle.

The conditions on the Home Orb were stabilized but the scarcity of breathable air was quickly becoming the most critical issue.

Nadia was sure her special project of doubling the size of the Confluence was the right focus. The team working on the ability to build a duplicate of the Confluence decided it would be more feasible to build an expanded Confluence having two parallel wheels. The Confluence would provide the base from which to build. Perhaps later when their building capabilities increased, building a separate ship would be feasible but at present they did not have the skills to accomplish the building of a second separate ship.

The work to construct the elevator system continued at full speed as they returned to the Home Orb. The meticulous detail of weaving a perfect pull line took up the attention of most of the Confluence crew. Every weaver had two quality inspectors. A flawless line of such length had never been produced. Each weaver wove for only one click then another weaver with their set of inspectors took the next click. There were only twenty qualified weavers and forty inspectors.

The weaving was continuous and never ceased.

Nadia proposed her new survival plan to Raulens, Keren, Lamins, and Milan. Her vision was to have all remaining Orbians come on board the Confluence. All the Orbian survivors would become space faring explores of the stars.

Their ability to expand their home was limited only by how fast they could gather and process the materials found all around them. They as Orbians could recover and when a habitable Orb with as much life potential as the Blue Orb and a comparable gravity to their Home Orb was found they could re-establish themselves. Until then they would expand their space vessel and make new ones as needed.

"Given the rapid depletion of the air on our Home Orb, this seems to me to be a very practical plan," Raulens responded.

"I get a little queasy thinking about spending the rest of my days in space but since that is where little Hope is, I am ready to give it a try," Milan replied.

Raulens and Keren took this proposal to the entire surviving group. The debate and discussion were still going on as Nadia headed back toward the Home Orb with the Confluence.

Young Hope and her playmate Hedris had the run of the Confluence. Two sitters were always watching out for them. Having the two youngsters running about on the Confluence seemed to give the crew a boost of energy. They were tolerated in almost all locations. Only the more dangerous areas and the area where the weaving of the pull line was being done were off limit.

Nadia made a point of spending as much time as possible with both of the two youngsters.

The completion of the pull cable occurred at the time of their arrival back to the Home Orb. A cheer rippled through the Confluence as the word of the completion became public.

Nadia had the cheer broadcast throughout the communication system. All the colonists sent in their congratulations.

The Raulens' and Milan colonists had already figured out that the success of the space elevator on their Home Orb would potentially lead to a similar success for them. Both colonies were ready to go back on board the Confluence. The struggles and obstacles they faced would never end. They wanted a home that offered some comfort and safety.

The navigation team brought the confluence into a low fast synchronous orbit twenty percent closer than the cable length. This gave them some ability to control the cable and the Confluence's position.

Their practice during the time at the Blue Orb now paid off. The Blue Orb had provided a practice ground that had a much stronger magnetic and gravitational field. The control systems had all been improved based on their learning. They had simulated their control system and practiced continually on the return voyage.

"Elevate me, take me up and down, ride the Confluator, ride me now," could be heard by anyone walking by the Confluence's control center. There was a heady feeling and a high level of confidence among the Confluence's navigators and pilots.

"I think we need to see what they are drinking," Lamens joked as he heard the rowdy exuberance.

Raulens discovered one of the rocket launch chambers was still useable. It made the perfect location to anchor the bottom side of the elevator. The elevator construction was shielded and when the time came, the lift cable would be lifted from this location out to the Confluence.

The lighter lines could be located in the maintenance areas and the final heavy-duty cable would be positioned out on the surface of the Orb.

Keren led a team to clear the tunnel leading to the launch chamber and to re-establish that specific elevator system to bring up materials to the chamber. This clearing of the path to the tube and the subsequent movement of the materials that would be raised to the Confluence took about half the time that the Confluence was taking to make its return trip.

"Every day I thank the designer of these exo-skeletons. They enable us to do the work of ten," Keren commented as he stepped out of his unit.

"I think the new suits and oxygen systems are on par to the exo-skeleton," Mislan replied as she greeted Keren.

"Yes, I agree. Together these two systems have enabled us to get all the materials moved into place. I hope there is enough room on the Confluence for all the materials we are staging," Keren continued.

Milan was in charge of the production of the large main and the required smaller pull cables. Every resource available in Ulm was brought to bear on this project.

It was becoming clear to everyone that life on the Orb was already slowly getting harder.

The remaining air on the planet was redistributing itself and getting thinner as this occurred. This made it harder to reclaim the needed volume for their survival. The original air compressors were not efficient enough to provide all the required compressed air.

"This space elevator idea and the Confluence's return can only be described as a small miracle," Triansa commented as she adjusted the compressor settings on one of the more efficient compressor models.

Nadia's idea of having all Orbians on the Confluence was slowly gaining popularity. After fourteen cycles the progress of the Home Orb survivors was flat. Life was improving but the long term seemed overwhelming. The continued discovery of the dead on the Home Orb made their existence morbid.

The space elevator and the promise of a stable life on the Confluence had rippled through the population.

They were ready for the ride up.

The Confluence navigators flaunted their capabilities. Their approach and positioning of the Confluence was flawless.

The team managing the pull line fired their small rocket and skillfully let out the line as it made its way to the surface. They were homing in on a beacon coming from the launch tube. The line pulled smoothly off the reel as it disappeared toward the surface.

Keren and a crew of six were out on the surface strategically spaced around the entrance to the launch tube. They questioned the ability of the controllers on the Confluence to hit the launch tube from such a far distance.

Keren and his team were out on the surface to make sure the line was brought into the tube.

The rocket pulling the cable down could be seen as a sparkle in the sky.

One of Keren's team was talking to the team on the Confluence. Amazingly, last minute firing adjustments placed the cable within several steps of the launch tube entrance.

The ground team quickly carried the missile and line to the edge of the tube and dropped it in. They simultaneously signaled for the line feed to stop.

Raulens team waiting in the tube removed the rocket and immediately connected the pull line to the next larger cable. The command to begin the pull up was sent. After an initial delay, the slack in the small cable was taken in and the larger cable began its journey up.

There was a cheer on the Confluence as the reel began to take the small line back in. Several other reels were available on which to wrap the next larger cable. The actual lift cable would be wound up on the exterior of the Confluences central section.

The pull up of the next size cables took several full work cycles. Finally, after three ever larger cables had been stored on separate spools, it was time for the heavy lift of the actual elevator cable.

The navigation team had allowed extra room in their altitude because they needed to periodically make adjustments as the weight of the cable affected their position. The higher gravity of the Blue Jewel had honed their skill and they were able to maintain their altitude within the required boundaries.

The energy required to hold the position of the Confluence would limit their ability to maintain the use of the elevator to no more than twenty work cycles.

Raulens had extended this time limit by planning to send fuel up from the Home Orb. "We have all the fuel you need. Your patience will run out before the fuel," he radioed up.

The survivors on the Home Orb knew this would most likely be the single time this connection would occur. The unanimous decision was to go on board the Confluence.

Every trip of the elevator would carry the maximum capacity of valuable materials and at least one hundred survivors.

Thirty trips were planned.

The elevator had a control team that would ride up and down for all the trips. This team managed the controls to keep the elevator from spinning or twisting. The upward speed was a constant fixed crawl. The first elevator ride up was of fuel and materials only.

Once it docked and was unloaded it immediately proceeded to descend at a rate five times faster than its upward climb speed.

The trips up and down though numbered, were constant and routine. The key materials going up were materials for the expansion of the Confluence. All plant and animal life represented on the Home Orb was brought up.

Milan and Triansa were coming up together.

Nadia stood inside the receiving station waiting for the door to open.

After so many Orbian cycles, she would get to see her mother again.

She held young Hope on her hips as the elevator was slowly pulled into the receiving area. The pressure between the elevator chamber and the Confluence was equalized and the door slowly slid open.

Milan was the first one out. She took in the scene of Nadia, Hope and Lamins standing together. She remembered the scene at their dinner table so long ago when they had first realized their world was coming to an end. Her wish to see Nadia have a family had been granted. Though she knew Raulens did not believe. She knew there must be some higher being looking down upon them.

Triansa and Milan stood together taking in the sight of their children and grandchild. They had talked about this moment for so many cycles that it now seem surreal.

They were frozen in place.

Nadia put Hope on the floor. Hope had heard about and seen pictures of her grandmothers and ran eagerly forward and jumped into both their arms.

Milan had brought up a small doll she had recovered from her home. It had been Nadia's favorite. She took it out and gave it to Hope.

Nadia recognized it and stood with tears in her eyes as she recognized her doll. She had forgotten her silent friend and now it would be Hope's friend.

They all joined together in one big huddle with arms around each other and Hope in the middle holding her new doll.

Nadia and Lamins led the way to the quarters prepared for their parents. Eventually, each would have a place similar to theirs. The amount of space for each family was limited but communal space was more abundant. Even then the space on the Confluence was considerably less than the new arrivals coming up from the Orb normally enjoyed.

The crew welcomed each of the survivors coming up from the Home Orb. They escorted each new arrival to the receiving area where they were greeted and shown to a temporary living area. Once everyone was on board the final living arrangements would be worked out.

New energy could immediately be felt on the Confluence.

Everyone coming on board commented on the great living conditions that the Confluence seemed to have.

Milan was immediately taken to the leader in charge of the gardens. The two had talked often and were very well acquainted with each other. Milan was somewhat of a legend to all on board. Those working in the gardens surrounded her and wanted her to inspect and give advice on what they were doing in their area.

Nadia left her mother in the gardens and went back to monitoring the lifts and understanding what materials were coming up.

Metals and key production units were the primary items being brought up. Abundant amounts of dried food were also high on the priority list. Cataloguing and storing the materials brought up took up the time between elevator arrivals. The central area slowly filled. Half of each connecting section was filled next. Finally, the outer areas of the wheel began to be filled. The fuel tanks were all topped off. The final loads included the historic physical books and materials from the Ulm University library.

Raulens would be among the last to ride up. His team was making the final adjustments to the cable system. If they ever came back in the future a guide cable could be sent down and guided through the giant ring at the base of the launch chamber. A cone was built around the ring. The line would slide to the center and through to the eye. Those above would then need to be able to connect to the ring to re-establish the connection from above. It would be fishing with a giant hook.

Raulens also sent up ten self-boring anchors. He had designed these so the Confluence could connect a space elevator to any surface they chose to. The anchors were designed to be attached at the end of the descending line and then its rotating screw head would rotate swiftly and pull the anchor down into the ground or the ice surface. This design assumed there would be no assistance at the anchor end.

Nadia and Lamens chose to descend on one of the last elevator rides down. They were greeted by Keren and Raulens. They had come down to understand the devastation the black void had inflicted.

Keren and Raulens guided them through the streets of Ulm. Many areas still remained closed. The entrances and doors to various chambers were already beginning to break down. Most of the support systems were no longer functional.

It was indeed a city of ghosts.

Nadia was shocked by the amount and extent of the devastation and the random nature of its destruction. She made it a point of asking to see the burial areas of the millions of fatalities. She and Lamens had brought a ceramic plaque showing the Confluence and a poem to commemorate dead.

It read,

Our Time Is Past

From Ancient roots,

    From times now past,

        We stay behind we are at rest.

Our brothers and sisters, journey on.

    They are alive.

        They are the last.

            They will remember us.

                They will sing our song.

Our time is past.

The plaque depicted the Home Orb, the collision with the void and the ravaging of the Orb. It had the position of the stars and other Orbs at the moment of the Confluence. Those finding the plaque would be able to determine when the event had occurred. Nadia hoped someday those from the Blue Jewel would make their way and find the plaque.

They returned to the elevator tube ready for the final ride up to the Confluence.

Chapter 21: Journey Out

They were silent on their ride up to the Confluence. They stared down and took in the devastated landscape.

"I see the path I use to walk when I went to the Observatory. I can see the Observatory shield. Those times now seem like a dream so far away and so impossible," Nadia said quietly.

"I know the hollow feeling. Keren and I have handled so many of the dead that we will live with their ghosts for the rest of our lives. Your success with the Confluence and those we sent up with you has been the inspiration for all of us. Thank you," Raulens said quietly as he took her hand.

Keren put his arms around Nadia's waist, "Little sister, Thank, you for looking out for me," he whispered through his tears.

Lamens joined them in their embrace and thanked then all.

When the elevator reached the Confluence, it was locked into its holder. The cable to the surface was maneuvered to the spool winder. The Confluence changed orientation so the cable would wind on the outside of the central rocket. The cable bolts at the Orb surface end were exploded and the cable came free from the ground anchor.

The release was somewhat of surprise, but the control system and team were able to respond to the outward surge.

It took three work cycles to slowly wind the cable up.

"I marvel at the skill this crew has mastered to maintain their orbital position as they reel in the elevator cable," Raulens said in praise.

"Lamens and Nadia were relentless in making us practice," one of the crew member piped in.

The new arrivals to the Confluence were greeted and welcomed by everyone on board.

The Evintons were as happy about Hope and about Lamins chance of having a family as Milan was about Nadia. They considered the chance to enjoy a grandchild and to see their son and daughter again a miracle. They would now travel through the Orb system to places they had never thought possible.

Everyone coming on board was asked to volunteer for some work area. Except for navigation and astronomy most of the new members were able to do much the same work they had been engaged in on the Home Orb. The living areas were assigned, and everyone moved into their new homes.

Soon after the Confluence pulled away from the Home Orb Nadia called her design team to review the expansion design.

This surprised Raulens and Keren. They had not anticipated such quick action. The design team had focused on doubling the Confluence in size. The design was based on the extension of the center rocket section and then building a replica of the rotating wheel. The building was planned to begin immediately. The goal was to have the new section completed by the time the Confluence reached the first colony on Milan.

Nadia asked Keren to lead the building of the new section of the Confluence.

"I am honored to be asked to be project leader and eagerly look forward to contributing to the team's success. However, let's progress more slowly. After reviewing these initial plans, I am sure Denal has been doing an excellent job filling this role. I suggest I come on board more slowly as an advisor and project reviewer. Let's keep the team as it is and let me just blend in," Keren smoothly guided his transition into the team.

"I see that you have perfected your political touch," Nadia commented later.

She showed Raulens the photos of the Blue Orb. There was a lifetime of analysis in reviewing the volume of pictures Nadia and her team had taken.

Each photo held information about the life on this robust environment. Most of the photos had been digitized and stored on the memory crystals. Raulens eagerly joined the team currently working on the review and analysis of the Blue Orb photos. He too had no desire to lead the team but would act in an advisory and analysis capacity. He was overwhelmed with the quantity and quality of all the photographs.

"Thank you for giving me such a fine present. This is such a relief from the work I have been doing in guiding the survival on the Home Orb," Raulens commented after his first review of the materials.

Milan joined the garden leadership team in an advisory role. She planned to spend most of her time with Hope, but her skills were sought by those managing the expansion and management of the gardens. The expansion of the Confluence meant a doubling of the gardens. The expansion provided the opportunity to expand the variety of the plants being cultivated. Milan had added at least one hundred new varieties of plants.

"We can't wait to get all these plants started. It is a shame that the live plants you had on the Orb could not have been transported up to us," one of the leaders commented.

"I was given the choice of bringing up the quizl or the live plants. I had to choose my friends," Milan replied jokingly.

She had actually cried about leaving her live plants, but she knew there was not enough time or energy to get them up to the Confluence. She had indeed chosen to bring every quizl that had been rounded up. She knew there were many more that had been left behind. She hoped they would be able to live out their lives in peace.

Nadia called all the leadership together to integrate the newly arrived among them. She asked each Confluence team to examine their area and define what they would need as the Confluence was doubled in size. The materials brought up from the Home Orb would be used to facilitate the immediate start of the expansion. The path through the debris orbit would be adjusted to ensure sufficient material was gathered to support the completion of the expansion.

Nadia had matured in her time as the survival leader of the Confluence. She made sure she surrounded herself with the best people she could, and she made sure these leaders engaged everyone in a positive, developmental way. They could not afford any issues to get in the way of the wellbeing of the Confluence as a whole.

The first priority was to expand the Confluence. This would enable it to increase the number of people it could comfortably support.

The news of the expansion and the ability for the Confluence to connect to the surface with its elevator gave the colonies on Milan the encouragement they needed. They were again struggling with the energy generation system. They would welcome the opportunity to get back on board the Confluence. They were drilling an additional energy well to sustain their meager survival environment. This was necessary to ensure their viability until the Confluence returned to pick them up. They saw the return of the Confluence as their only hope.

The colony on Raulens was in better shape. However, they too immediately embraced the idea of moving up to the Confluence. They remembered a much better life there then they had been able to establish in their slowly sinking colony. They put all their energy into the preparation for pickup. They had not shown so much enthusiasm since they had first landed.

Nadia established two rescue teams to determine how the Confluence would accomplish the pickup of the two colonies and to work the pickup details with each of the colonies. The two teams would coordinate their learning, but they would each manage their specific rescue pickups. This would include the anchoring technique for the elevator system.

Raulens was asked to provide periodic technical review to both teams.

The colony out on Hope was doing better than the rest. It was now living in the expanded area at the base of their deep bore tunnel. They had an abundance of energy and were doing well. They were aware of the outward journey of the Confluence and the pickup of the first two colonies. They decided to leave the resolution of the question as to their desire for pick up unanswered until the time the Confluence was on its way out to them. This was at least five Orb Cycles in the future. Much could happen in such a long period of time. They concentrated their efforts on making their colony as livable as possible.

The Confluence entered the debris field where the fifth orb should have been, as a single structure. The goal was to leave the debris belt with the Confluence doubled in size. They would make one complete cycle in the debris field. It would come in as the Confluence and depart as the Confluence ll.

The production systems for the expansion of the Confluence were put online. There was a total of ten brick fabrication lines that would work around the cycle. The additional Orbians meant that the staffing was enough to keep the systems constantly producing. The two sections sacrificed earlier to the make the balancing ring were rebuilt. The center section was expanded with the materials brought up from the Home Orb. New T sections were produced and added in a balanced fashion. Construction was always paced and controlled to keep everything in physical balance.

The counterbalance weight for the elevator system was also used to counterbalance the additional weight being distributed during construction.

Keren became one of the busiest of all the leaders as he and Denal guided the construction. The two had learned to work together well and they had developed and were executing their production plan. Since the work went on around the cycle this arrangement meant that one of them was always on duty.

Nadia and Milan spent a great deal of time together taking care of Hope and Hedris. This was time neither had expected to have together. Nadia knew her mother was near the end of her life. Hope was the spark keeping the fire burning. Each day was a treasure to be put into the heart. The family resurrected the practice of having their end of cycle meal together. Each day Milan would bring in some fresh fruit from the gardens.

Triansa and Kinser joined these family meals. Triansa was often the preparer of some special dish. Just as often one of her Chef students would bring in a new dish they had prepared.

At one of the dinners Keren's mate Mislan shared she would deliver a child on the way out to Milan. This was good news since it indicated the conditions on the Confluence provided the necessary protection allowing new births to occur.

"I am too old to be wishing for more, but I am too young to miss out on seeing another grandchild," Milan whispered to Raulens.

The stay in the debris field fell just short of a full Home Orb Cycle. Every conceivable internal space and even the external space between the central spokes of the Confluence were filed with raw materials. The living space had temporarily been cut in half and filled with the raw materials scavenged from the debris belt.

"Do we really need all of this?" Keren asked as he toured with Nadia.

"That is a good question. However, my question is better. Is it enough?" Nadia replied with a smile.

The Confluence II would be commissioned as it sped outward toward the giant Orb and the colony of Milan.

"We will officially commission the Confluence II when the external work is complete. This will be a ceremony to be held when we arrive at Milan. The internal work will be undertaken on the way out to Hope," Nadia announced to the Confluence Crew.

The new sections of the Confluence II were superior in quality and design. Nadia had her design team working on the plans for the remodeling of the older sections. The remodeling of the original sections would take place after the pickup of the colonists on Milan and Raulens.

She also asked Keren to lead the development of plans for Confluence III. She wanted one more wheel to be added on the way out to Hope.

This would mean two thousand beings for each wheel. This was a density of two hundred beings per section. The space would be adequate and the open path around each wheel would provide room for all to walk and relax.

Then in the near future they could add yet another wheel to make Confluence IV. This expansion would probably be after her time, but she wanted to provide the vision of a long-term existence for the next generation. Their origin was on the Home Orb their future would be space faring beings.

"We have been devastated but we are not defeated," Nadia thought as she walked around the gardens and watched the others doing the same.

Chapter 22: The Long Road

The journey time to Milan proved long enough to have the second wheel complete and ready for use. Upon the arrival to Milan a commissioning ceremony to rename the Confluence was carried out.

"The Confluence II will now bring up the colonists that the Confluence I so recklessly lowered to the surface," Nadia announced as the space elevator anchor was lowered to the surface and fired into the ice.

It hit the target zone and a crew on the ground secured the anchor and the initial pull line.

The Confluence was able to position itself one third the distance established at the Home Orb. This meant a much shorter ride on the elevator. The primary focus was getting the colonist up to the Confluence.

The effect of the Giant Orb made keeping the Confluence in position more difficult than at the Home Orb. There was a constant need for adjustments. The trips up were packed to capacity and the trips down went as fast as they possibly could. The last load included all the top end technology equipment as well as the few remaining colonists. Most of the materials including the valuable sections of the Confluence were left on the surface. It was too dangerous to spend the time trying to retrieve more. After the final run, the ground anchor was blown from the ice and cable retrieval initiated.

They had made the recovery in only three work cycles.

The Confluence II immediately began its outward journey to intersect Raulens. The anchor navigation team was mentally exhausted from the tension of keeping the Confluence in position. They were happy to have the normal navigation team take over.

Material collection was again a key focus. The external areas around the spokes had been modified to act as material storage areas. There was even an initial segregation screening process that separated and stored like materials together. On the way to Raulens, the material gathering team participated with the navigation team to optimize the raw material gathering process.

The colonists up from Milan were amazed at what they found on the Confluence II. They had left a sparse crowded environment. They returned exhausted by their own experience and found the comfort and the environment they had forgotten ever existed. They walked around for several cycles marveling at the changes they found.

They made a point specifically of specifically thanking everyone they met. They sought out Nadia and gave her hugs and thanked her for having inspired them to survive and then rescuing them.

Nadia had tears of joy at each of these meetings. She would forever cherish the moments.

"Thank you for surviving long enough for me to rescue you," Nadia announced to the Milan members as she quickly integrated them into the work teams. She wanted them acclimated and ready to receive the colonist from Raulens.

The Confluence II continued gathering material as it moved through the various levels of material making up the rings around the giant orb. The navigation team had developed a high degree of material collection capability. The material bins were slowly filling and being processed as the Confluence II went into orbit around Raulens.

Keren and his expansion team were busy preparing for the next phase of expansion. The production systems creating the ceramic building blocks were operating at full capacity. Once the Raulens colonists were picked up construction on the third wheel would begin. Scheduled completion was upon arrival at Hope.

The pickup on Raulens was easier than at Milan. The force of the Giant Orb was not as overwhelming. The Raulens pickup lasted longer, and they were able to recover almost all the materials sent down. This was a plus for the Confluence II and to the progress of the construction of the Confluence III.

A large amount of ice was brought up to replenish the water supply. This provided additional chemicals and other minerals found in the ice. The biological learning and the extraction of the minerals gave the scientist new understanding about both the Milan and Raulens moons.

The arrivals coming up from Raulens were no less surprised than those who had come up from Milan. It was an overwhelming relief to be free of the fight of keeping some critical system running with the minimum of resources.

The Confluence II was currently filled to the brim with raw materials.

The two thousand new members brought the total population of the Confluence to six thousand. This made for a full but comfortable living situation. It was good that their race preferred closeness over too much space.

Young Hope was now three cycles old. She and her young friend were the two oldest of the now six offspring. They were active and always together. Everyone humored them and they had the run of the entire Confluence II.

Hope was excited about the journey out to the colony with her name. She would be five when they arrived.

Just when Nadia began to be worried about the fertility issue, she learned there were at least six additional females expecting young. She asked Mislan and a team of other female members to determine the number and timing of the new births. They would need to limit and to space the births to ensure the population would not explode but would have a uniform age profile.

She immediately saw the need for a fourth wheel. The sixth orb also had a debris ring. The Confluence II would once again need to gather the materials for expansion. She wondered how large the Confluence would be able to grow. She called together her design team and requested they not only study a fourth wheel but also enclosing the space between each wheel.

The Confluence was becoming a massive structure. Interestingly the fuel required to keep it in motion went up as the cube root of the weight. This relationship proved to be manageable and the original fuel tank sizes were adequate. She put the expansion of these tanks as a primary consideration. The material from the rocket sections brought up from Raulens was allocated to be used to build the expansion of the fuel tanks.

The visit to Hope would be an opportunity to stock up on the fuel. Creating it from the raw materials collected as they moved through space was feasible and doable, but Hope provided a wealth of fuel. Nadia wanted the maximum fuel possible to be brought up as insurance for the long journey beyond the Orbital system.

Raulens was leading the visual exploration of every major Orb and all the objects circling them. His team was one hundred in number. They worked around the cycle. Observing, cataloguing, and publicizing their learning kept the teams busy. Their information board was a daily stopping place for everyone. Nadia spent a few hours each day with this team. She, however, made the rounds with Lamins to review all the work going on to get the Confluence III built.

Keren and his construction crew also worked around the cycle. He had four teams. One team was always on a recovery cycle. This allowed the work to make rapid progress. His work force was more than half the population.

Keren was in his element. He thanked Nadia almost every day for rescuing him from the Home Orb. Nadia always made a small rebuttal joke about getting even for sending her out on her own.

Milan was in her element. Early each cycle she would relax and play with Hope and Hedris. She would pass them off to Nadia or the other care takers and tour the gardens. She was revered for her knowledge and always had a cast accompany her as she inspected and tended to her favorite plants. They were of course all her favorites. She was forever planning another improvement and had a bevy of co-conspirators all trying to come up with the next big plant improvement. She encouraged all of them. She knew the gardens were a critical factor in ensuring the continuity of those living on the Confluence.

A little over half the way to Hope, Nadia surprised the leadership team with a proposed change to the order of growth and construction of the Confluence III. Her design team had developed a plan to enclose the three wheels and create a giant central area to serve as the fuel reservoir. This massive area would ensure the Confluence would be able to store enough fuel to last three hundred orb cycles.

It was the first time the leadership team questioned Nadia's suggestion.

Nadia had come prepared for this reaction. Before bringing the topic into the team she had worked with Raulens and a small team to determine how long a trip to the next orb system would take. Raulens estimate was two hundred fifty orb cycles. This estimate was what made Nadia decided that they would need the quantity of fuel she was asking for. She wanted to ensure the success of the next leg of the Orbian Journey.

She now shared the long-term vision of journey the Orbians would be undertaking. The discussion went on most of the work cycle.

Keren was eloquent in his support for Nadia's vision and the practicality of creating the fuel reservoir. His description of the journey and the life on board the Confluence guided the discussion to agreement. His ability to take the opposing view, agree with it and then show why it should be let go proved to be the process that aligned everyone to Nadia's request.

"Thanks for watching out for your little sister," Nadia whispered as she gave Keren a hug.

Nadia then shared the drawing and the artist's rendition of the Confluence IV Prime. The ship was indeed becoming a massive structure.

Keren became active in reviewing and modifying the design. He was instrumental in ensuring adequate strengthening and the addition of flow inhibitors to the design of the fuel tanks.

He guided the design team in evaluating the best storage techniques. There would be several elements to the fuel. They would be stored separately and only combined when it came time for them to be used. This would make the storage much safer. The space in question would actually be multiple tanks. The fuel to be brought up from Hope would be processed, separated, and put into the separate tanks and later they would be pulled in the right proportion for use.

The colony on Hope was contacted and engaged in the discussion. This brought the colonist on Hope to their decision point. When they learned their race was departing from this orb system. All of them agreed that they did not want to be left behind. They voted unanimously to join the Confluence III.

"I am relieved that the Hope colonists reached this conclusion. It would have been very hard to leave them behind. However, I was prepared to do so," Nadia confided to the family.

Keren laughed and said that he would not want to be someone that opposed her desires.

The colonists on Hope began to immediately separate the fuel into the desired constituents. They would have much of the fuel ready by the time the Confluence was in orbit with them. This separation on the surface made it much safer to bring up to the Confluence III.

The Elevator system was not sufficient to load the amount of fuel desired in a reasonable time frame. To load the planned amount of fuel a series of pumping stations would need to be established. This also meant a very long series of tubes connecting the pumping stations. The design for this system went in circles. The pumping station idea died when the number of required pumps was calculated. Finally, a series of crawling bubbles was proposed. It was in essence a series of small elevators continuously crawling up one cable to the Confluence. Once empty they would free fall down a second cable.

These small bubbles would crawl up on cables positioned just outside the diameter of the main elevator and deliver their fuel to the suction tubes.

The main elevator would also bring up fuel every time it made a trip. However, its primary mission would be to bring up minerals and materials from the surface.

Nadia made a trip down to the surface with Raulens and Keren. They traveled down to the living quarters far below the surface. Clearly this colony had done well. However, the environment was not very favorable. The system required constant pumping to keep it from filling with the liquid of the Orb.

The unanimous vote to come up to the Confluence was understandable. The long-term risk of the environment was obvious.

Nadia was relieved to have been able to retrieve all the survivors. Their risk and perils had weighed heavy on her. Now all the Orbians faced the same challenge. Her newly established leadership team all shared in the decisions about their final destination.

Keren was engaged with Raulens, Kinser, Neihen, Milan and Triansa in defining a constitution that would guide the day to day lives of those on board. An internal government was to be established. This government would be separate from the control and the guidance of the Confluence IV Prime spaceship.

The new constitution and the renaming of the Confluence III to the Confluence IV Prime was to take place once the ship released itself from the surface of Hope.

Each cycle Nadia watched as the fuel tanks slowly filled. The Navigation team members were now experts at holding their station in synchronous orbit. Nadia watched as the indicators on the fuel tanks finally indicated they were full. The metals and other valuable surface materials filled all other storage compartments.

The Confluence IV Prime was now ready to continue the voyage.

There was one more ceremony she had planned before her race left the Grand Orb system.

The white ceramic container designed to hold the history cube and the visual instructions on how to activate the cube lay before her on the table.

Raulens and Milan had been the primary organizers and designers of the history container.

The primary item was the history cube but there were physical etchings on a ceramic surface depicting each of the species of their Orb.

There was an etching of the Grand Orbital system and all the orbs around the central Orbit.

There was one ceramic square with the symbols of their language and the numbering system they used.

There was one physical sample of each surface their species had touched in the orb system.

Milan was carefully placing each article into position. Once everything was in place a sap like liquid was poured in to encapsulate the contents. This sap would remove all air and encapsulate the items in a chemically neutral environment.

A liquid ceramic was spread around the edge of the chest and the lid was lowered into place. The ceramic spread would create a molecular bond as the lid and the rest of the container essentially became a single object. The bonding action would take place over several cycles.

Once done the ceramic box would last for an unknown but extremely long time period.

"I hope at least several millions of cycles," Nadia thought to herself as she thought back to the life currently rising up on the Blue Jewel. She wished that the Jewel and the eventual rise of intelligence would someday reach Hope and find out about the Orbians and their valiant effort at survival.

Nadia took the carbon made from plant materials and put it into the vertical hole located on the top corner of the container. She lowered the carbon rod into the sap like liquid to encapsulate it as well. A black ceramic plug was fused into place to seal this age sensor. She hoped the future discovers would know how to determine the age of the chest.

She expected it to be several million cycles before the chest would be found.

This was the third marker Nadia had planted for the next intelligence of this orbital system.

She had no doubt the rich in life Blue Jewel would produce sentient beings. She hoped they would discover the previous existence of the Orbians and in some distant future the two intelligences of this Orbital System could connect.

She and Raulens went down to the surface of Hope one last time to put the chest into its holder. They had chosen the elevator anchor as the location to put the chest. The anchor and the chest were the two objects they felt would last the longest time.

Their Journey's End was somewhere out beyond their Grand Orb System. It was beyond their time. It was in the future of their race.

Nadia composed a final goodbye song for her Grand Orb System. It was a song she would leave to those in the future.

<u>Our Song, So Bittersweet</u>

From Ancient roots,

    From times now past,

        We on this journey,

           The few,

               The last.

We sing a song,

    In memory

        To all before us,

           To us, the remaining few,

It is a sad song.

No tears,

No laughter,

No one living left behind.

We are the last.

Our time here is past.

Our future is out, out into the vast

The vast expanse

The expanse of space and time.

Nadia called her team together. The next part of the journey would be so long none of those beginning would be alive at the end. The journey to the next closest potential system was about three hundred cycles. This was a journey of about ten generations.

Truly, they would be space beings when the next potential Home Orb would be reached. There was no doubt the Orbians would survive and excel. They had traveled their Grand Orb System in the most trying of times and in the most embryonic conditions.

Nadia had successfully led her race up from oblivion. She was already revered in her own time. The succeeding generations would expand her aura until she would eventually be a full legend.

The trip out would be long. At times it would be trying but mostly it would be long. The key would be the constant study of the Universe around them. To be constantly learning and developing knowledge was now the main purpose of the remaining Orbians.

Nadia then gave the command to depart.

<u>Epilogue</u>

More than two hundred and fifty million years was to pass before once again the confluence of the Solar System and the Black Hole would occur. This was the time it took the solar system to make one rotation around the center of the Milky Way.

The immense passage of time hid the evidence of the Orbian existence.

Nadia's Orb, Mars still circled the sun on its lonely journey.

And the Earthlings asked if there might have been the existence of life on Mars.

Earth had indeed developed intelligent beings. It had lived through numerous cataclysmic events. The single continent had split, and the Teutonic plates had drifted to form a totally new land arrangement. It was still a Blue Jewel in the solar system, and it still teamed with life.

It was no longer the land that Nadia had seen or studied. Most of that life had perished and been replaced by the elements of life that survived through the many challenges the Earth experienced.

The planet known as Mars was seen as a barren, lifeless planet to the Earthlings. They finally reached the stage where they too were capable of space travel. They too struggled with the intense radiation that the Earth's strong magnetic field shielded them from.

They were slowly able to learn what the Orbians had learned about the solar system that surrounded them. It was almost a duplication of learning that the Orbians had gone through.

The evidence of this periodic interaction of the solar system and the black hole was evident in the rubble where a fifth inner planet should have formed. It was evident in the condition of Mars. However, there was no context that provided mankind with reference to make sense of the damage inflicted on the solar system. They thought it was the random nature of solar system formation.

They had no idea that a small blackhole was awaiting their arrival.

Savitar is the continuing story of the solar system's interaction with this small black hole that exists on the edge of the Milky Way.

This time it was the Earth that would face the same fate as those billion of Orbians on Mars.

This time the question was, would the Earth with its ten billion people survive?

The End

Preview of: Savitar

Chapter 1:Discovery

The threat of Earth's total destruction startled and confounded Zack. His initial comprehensive analysis confirmed his conclusion.

He thought through how to get verification from his analysis support team.

The disappearance of the asteroid he had been following came as a surprise and at first, he had assumed it was data error.

He had used three additional reliable sources of the data and the result was the same.

He had he discussed this with Craig, his partner. He assumed some sort of error and had discounted the finding.

Zack left shortly after the other team members. He went about his normal workout still chewing on the problem as he ran laps. He showered went home and went to bed.

By three in the morning, he gave up trying to sleep. He decided to get up for an early morning breakfast and went to a nearby all night diner that he often frequented.

"Hi Arlene, let's start with a cup of coffee and then I will see what else I get," Zack said as he sat down at the counter.

He took in the rest of the diner. There was an old man sitting over a cup of coffee but otherwise the place was empty. This was just a small hole in the wall place. He wondered how they made enough money to stay open.

After his breakfast, Zack left the diner, crossed the street, and went down into the subway. The walk to his office took him by a lush rose garden and tree lined park where he often went to eat his lunch. So early in the morning it loomed grey and more foreboding than usual. He figured it was the early morning hour and his state of mind.

Once he reached the office, he gathered his material for the normal morning analysis planning meeting. He was trying to figure out the best way to get the team to verify his findings.

When Craig came in, he sat down at his desk and looked over and declared that he had a miserable night and was upset about the analysis.

He came into the meeting in an ugly mood. He had reached the conclusion the team had made an analysis or observation error.

Zack knew Craig had come to the wrong conclusion, but he decided against arguing.

"How the hell can we lose a ten-mile-long asteroid?" Craig barked at the observation and analysis team.

Zack observed that Craig was talking to the team but looking directly at him.

"I want you to find out where we went wrong and I want you to find that dam asteroid," he continued

Zack knew what they would find but he decided to keep his mouth shut. There was no use arguing with his partner and mentor when he was mad.

He had now worked with Craig for almost ten years. Zack knew his own conclusion put him at the freaky fringe of scientific theory.

He needed independent verification and Craig's demands would accomplish that.

Zack decided to spend his time putting more detail to a solution his sleepless mind had come up with. He took his computer, a drawing pad and pencil and headed out to see if the rose garden in the park would help his thinking. He hoped it would provide the grounding that he felt he might have lost.

Until a few years ago, Zack had been Dr. Craig Garrity's sole assistant. He and Craig had spent six years using land and orbital telescopes in radio, light, and infrared technology to look back in time.

They studied the specific location of Earth in space over its billions of years of life and correlated these positions with the various periods of the extinction of life.

They found evidence of bombardment from debris fields in space leading to the periods of great extinction. Their work received wide recognition and Zack got his PhD in Astronomical History. This was a unique PhD that Zack with the support of Dr. Garrity had designed.

Zack remembered the day he, Dr. Garrity and a NASA representative met to discuss the possibility of getting funding to look ahead to where the Earth was going.

Dr. Garrity connected looking ahead to NASA's research in how to protect the Earth from another asteroid like the one that had killed off the dinosaur. He made an outstanding business arrangement.

He and Zack set up a firm to search ahead to the space into which Earth was heading. The government would provide the computing, analysis resources and office space. Together with NASA they set up a program they named "Pathfinder." Dr. Garrity enrolled his, across the world, network of acquaintances in the effort. All the major observatories were linked to Pathfinder's data banks. All orbiting telescopes were engaged. This was a winning arrangement for everyone involved.

Zack came up with the idea to enroll home PC users to help in the analysis. He designed and had an Analysis App programmed that could be downloaded to a personal computer. It could be activated and then do analysis in the background. This was a big hit with the general public. Junior high and high school students seemed to especially like the App. Many used the App on their i-phones. There were enough users that it provided a big chunk of the required data analysis

Since the Earth rotated around the Sun and the Sun traveled on the outer edges of the Milky Way, and the Milky Way was itself speeding away from the center of the Universe, determining where and how to look was a challenge for a host of astronomers, physicists, and mathematicians.

It took almost a year to develop a model for Earth's journey with enough detail to enable them to analyze the potential threats coming at them through space.

It was a multi-dimensional time and space analysis.

Zack new how easy it was to get lost when doing the analysis and then putting it to practical use to visually look ahead through a telescope. He and he network supporting him were doing this visually, in infrared and with radio signals.

Zack quickly recognized the necessity and the depth of the government financial pocket as they hired hundreds of data processors.

The data displaying a specifically defined signature was quickly processed.

Other, less-promising data was put in a large database and was slowly fed out to all the App users. These users downloaded small segments of it to their PC's or their i-phones. The analysis program chunked away. The chunks showing promise, from this second level of analysis, were highlighted by the apt and passed back up to the program analysts for more detailed analysis.

The disappearance of one three-mile wide by ten-mile-long asteroid slated for a close pass of Earth affirmed the value of all the tedious analysis that had been done.

The previous day Zack had reviewed the data and the visual record being made of the asteroid. He watched as the asteroid changed course, then seemed to stop and disappear.

He sat and did an initial sketch of his idea. Taking his work to the park had been a good idea. He was able to do an initial drawing and then put together the equation that he would complete to determine if he had any hope of making his idea real.

He walked back to the office and as he entered, he was immediately face with a still upset partner.

"How in the hell can we lose a ten-mile-long asteroid?" Craig asked again in consternation.

His confidence in the team was taking a beating at the moment. He was sure some mistake in data analysis had occurred.

Zack decided to continue to develop and work on his own analysis. He had come up with his own alarming conclusion and was quietly working on its proof and a potential solution.

Craig and the analysis team were focused on the period leading up to the disappearance. They requested back up data from all participating observatories. Craig ran through the analysis himself and reviewed the visuals. He pointed all telescopes to the last location of the asteroid. He had data collected in all the frequencies possible.

His analysis confirmed the disappearance. The asteroid began going off its course and then it seemed to stop. Finally, it slowly began to disappear. Infrared data showed the asteroid give out its last signature as it disappeared.

It was the dying signature of an object being consumed by a black hole!

Zack had been waiting all day for Craig to reach the point when he finished his analysis. He had meanwhile researched the conclusion he had reached the night before. He had found reference to his specific conclusion. Albert Einstein himself had predicted the existence of this find.

"What is your conclusion," Craig looked up and asked from across the office they shared?

"You seem to already know. When did you figure it out," Craig asked as he turned away from his computer and looked at Zack across the room?

"I figured it out yesterday before going home. It kept me up all night." Zack replied quietly.

"You find a black hole in the path of the solar system, and you keep quiet," Craig said with a shake of his head?

Sometimes he wondered about his young partner. He was brilliant but sometimes he was too polite.

"Would you have done anything differently since this morning if I had argued that it was not the analysis but a black hole," Zack said standing up to get another cup of coffee?

He asked if Craig would have accepted the concept of a small black hole waiting ahead in the path of the solar system. You know as well as I that small black holes are supposed to have ceased to exist at least a billion years ago.

After some discussion he and Craig decided they would need the independent confirmation of at least three other independent global teams. Craig would contact the teams and asked for their independent analysis of the missing asteroid

He sat down took a sip of his coffee and pulled up the analysis he had spent his time on.

"We not only have found a black hole. We have found one directly in the path of the solar system. More specifically it is one with which Earth is on a collision course with," Zack said as he put his analysis up on the large flat screen the two shared.

He had developed a rough drawing of the situation.

"How long do we have," Craig asked as he looked at the sketch?

"We have roughly four years until the edge of the solar system reaches the black hole and about seven years until it intersects Earth's orbit," Zack replied

I am ninety nine percent sure that Earth will be direct hit on this black hole. The hole is stationary. The solar system is approaching it on a collision course.

"Is there anything else you know that I should know," Craig asked?

"Yes, but I'm not talking until after our dinner. Emily made us promise to be on time and personally I love her cooking and don't intend to be late," Zack replied as he powered down his laptop and put it away in his briefcase.

Craig followed suit and the two walked out to his car.

"Welcome, I am surprised you two are early. There is beer or wine in the fridge. Go in the den. I'll call you when dinner is ready," Emily said as she greeted them.

Zack always made sure to be on time for Emily's dinners. She had trained as a chef and always served the most delicious dishes. He could not understand how Craig kept himself in such good shape. He figured he would be one hundred pounds heavier if Emily was his wife.

They had just finished the Modelo when Emily called them to dinner.

It was a rule that they did not discuss business at the dinner table, so the talk was about Emily's day.

Zack did share that the roses in the park were blooming and that there seemed to be several new types that had been planted.

"Emily that was another one of your marvelous dinners. We were early because I declined to engage your husband with any business when I realized we might be late for this treat," Zack said in praise as he sat back and sipped on the coffee that Emily had served.

"You two go into the living room. I will bring in some more coffee and a few cookies," Emily said as she got up to clean the table.

Both Zack and Craig carried their dishes over to the kitchen sink before going into the living room.

Afterwards they sat in front of the gas fireplace with a cup of coffee and some of Emily's cookies.

He had tried to think of a more persuasive way to say it, but he just blurted it out.

"I have a way to capture the black hole and move it out of Earth's path," Zack said.

He stopped and sipped on his cup of coffee and watched for Craig's reaction.

"Capture a black hole. Even if you can, what are you going to do once you capture it?" Craig asked with a chuckle as he contemplated the impossibility of such a task.

He really enjoyed the creativity that his star pupil and friend would periodically display. However, this was a little beyond the normal, it was a little on the crazy side.

He figured it was probably the caffeine from all the coffee Zack drank. He knew it was not drugs, but he would have believed so if he had not known his partner for so long.

"I am going to use the blackhole as the center of a giant spaceship. It will provide the gravity and the power for this spaceship," Zack replied quietly.

He was aware of Craig's skepticism, but he was sure of his idea and that he knew how to build the spaceship.

He had spent the day on the analysis of the power of this small black hole. He had concluded that it could be contained in a magnetic bottle.

He knew Craig was not yet understanding or accepting this as a serious suggestion.

"Tell me more," Craig said as he leaned forward to see if Zack was serious.

And by the tone of his voice, Craig thought Zack was serious.

"Here, let me show you," Zack said as he powered up his laptop.

He showed Craig his power analysis and a potential way to bottle the black hole.

They got into some serious and deep discussion.

Zack was surprised when he realized it was past two in the morning.

"Its lucky tomorrow is Saturday we should probably go to bed," Zack said.

He realized how tired he was. He was sapped.

"You're welcome to use the guest room." Craig said as he too realized how tired he was.

Emily had said good night when she brought in the coffee and cookies. That had been more than four hours earlier.

Craig was now hooked on Zack's idea. It would take a lot of additional analysis and design work, but the idea seemed plausible.

He once again was humbled by Zack's uncanny ability to cut through a monumental problem in a simple direct approach.

Zack accepted using the guest room. He made quick work of getting asleep.

It seemed that having someone accept his discovery and his solution as plausible had released his anxiety and he did not wake up until he her Emily's call for breakfast.

He looked at the clock and it was past nine-thirty.

"I let the two of you sleep in this morning.

I must be the only woman jealous of a former male student, for keeping my husband out all night.

What were the two of you talking about for so long," Emily joked.

She had taken Zack under her wing and thought of him almost as a younger brother. She had hosted Zack's parents on the ribbon cutting ceremony when Craig and Zack opened their current business.

"Well in all truthfulness, if I or Zack were to tell you, we would all have to be shot," Craig said giving Emily a good morning kiss while giving her pat on her behind.

He was not ready to tell anyone about this situation. Emily worried about threatening rainstorms. He was not about to mention Earth's potential doom idly or casually.

"Zack and I are going to have to work this weekend. We have a situation needing immediate attention. We need to prepare some presentation for this coming Monday or Tuesday.

The two left after a quick breakfast and went into the office.

Craig and Zack sat in their office reviewing what they had learned. The blackhole was not a collapsed star. The black hole was much too small. Instead, they theorized that it was material compressed by the original big bang formation of the universe that had made this relatively small black hole.

They wondered how it could maintain itself. Theoretically it took a much larger amount of mass to form and then maintain a black hole. This small but deadly one had absorbed or sucked in an asteroid almost ten miles in length and three miles wide. It seemed that it sustained itself by taking in these smaller chunks of matter.

Earth was too large to be sucked in, but an encounter with even a small blackhole would create havoc and have a dramatic impact. They theorized Earth's atmosphere, and its water would be stripped, and the event would likely disrupt the planet's orbit.

Zack postulated Mars might have experienced this same black hole in the distant past. He also pointed to the debris out past the orbit of Mars where a fifth planet should have formed. \

The cycle around the edge of the Milky Way was roughly once every two hundred fifty million years. Perhaps the Solar System had previously had multiple encounters with this black hole. Or perhaps there were other similar black holes in the galaxy. If his theory proved to be true, it would solve the long-discussed mystery of why Mars lost most of its atmosphere and its water.

"If we want to survive this encounter, we need to martial Earth's resources and take immediate action. How are we going to pull this off," Zack voiced his concern as he sat looking at the screen?

"I will contact the President and set up a meeting to brief him," Craig said.

Zack knew about Craig's friendship with the President. The two had grown up in the same neighborhood, attended school together and had both graduated from MIT. Craig had been an active campaigner for the newly elected President. Even so he was still surprised to see Craig calling the President on a Saturday.

Even so, Zack found it amazing that Craig could just dial him at a moment's notice.

"Yes, please tell him it's Dr. Craig Garrity and I have information critical to the well-being of the nation." Craig spoke into the phone.

He hung up.

"Let's see if Dan call's me back. He told me I could call him at any time." Craig said as he looked over and smiled at Zack.

A few moments later the phone rang. Craig put it on the speaker phone, but he put his finger to his lips and pointed to Zack.

"Well, I just left my daughter's swim meet. How are things with you and Emily," the President said in friendly tone?

"Emily is fine.

However, I really am calling about a very serious threat to the Earth. I want to review it with you this coming week. Please listen to me personally. Afterwards you can unleash all of your technical resources to verify what I tell you. Can you get me on your agenda," Craig replied more seriously?

"Yes, I will see you. Let's make it Monday at lunch. You know you have ruined my weekend with this. Should I pray in church tomorrow," the President replied?

"Thank you and yes several prayers would be appropriate," Craig responded.

"Wow, I never would have dreamt it would have been this easy to get to talk to and see the President," Zack said in amazement after Craig hung up the phone.

"Well getting Dan to listen will not be the issue. He just got sworn in. As you know I attended his inauguration.

Getting him to take immediate action and making it stick may be more of an issue. However, Dan has a history of making things move and getting things done. Let's get our presentation outlined and fleshed out. We don't want to blow this presentation," Craig said quietly.

Zack spent the rest of the morning working on his concept and preparing a draft of the presentation he had wanted.

Craig was reviewing the slides and adding the verbiage in the notes section of the presentation.

It was late Saturday afternoon when a of limo stopped in the parking lot of the office. Two black vans were parked on either side of a long stretch limo car.

Zack was shocked when he looked up to see two very serious men enter the room with their badges out.

"FBI is there anyone else here?" he asked looking around.

"We are the only ones," Zack replied thinking it was obvious no one else was in the room.

"How can we help you," Craig inquired.

"It's clear," the second agent said into his phone. The two stepped forward and to the side.

The president walked in.

"I couldn't wait until Monday. I know you wouldn't call me on something trivial. You are tracking a close encounter asteroid. Is it on a collision course?" the President asked as he came in.

Craig looked at the two agents.

"Are they cleared for all information," Craig inquired?

"Gentlemen, please give us a few moments alone," the President said to the two agents.

Once the door closed Craig stood up.

"Dan thanks for coming. Let me introduce you to Dr. Zackary Milton. He made the discovery we are going to tell you about. He has also proposed a solution to this problem. I am relieved to be able to put this in your capable hands. Zack, you tell the story," Craig said as he shook hands with the President.

Zack was a little unnerved.

"Mr. President...

"Please call me Dan," the President interrupted as he accepted a cup of coffee from Craig.

"Dan, there is a black hole directly in the path of the Solar system and it will be in Earth's orbit in about six years. Thursday, we witnessed it swallow the near pass asteroid we have been tracking," Zack spoke slowly and clearly.

He was trying to be as clear and as direct as possible. He wanted the President to understand the critical need for immediate action.

"You don't pull any punches. What kind of damage are we talking about," the President inquired?

"Well, this is a small black hole. It theoretically should have ceased to exist several billion years ago. Our solar system seems to be one source of its sustenance. It is too small to ingest the Earth but that won't do us any good.

It will likely leave Earth in the same condition we find Mars today. It would strip away the atmosphere, our oceans, everything on the surface," Zack replied.

"Here let me show you the pictures we have of it swallowing the asteroid," Zack continued.

"This is going to take more than a prayer in church. What is the solution you have come up with," the President inquired?

This time Zack pulled out his notebook.

"I was getting ready to put this into a graphics package. You're about a day early for anything more than my hand drawing. My calculations are all in my computer and of course they will take additional checking, but I am confident I have the right scale for the size of this solution," Zack said as he turned to the page with the sketches of the capture device.

"Dan, the dimensions of this capture device are at the limits of what is feasible with our current technology. It is doable but it will take the concerted effort of all the resources of the Earth.

The inner sphere is fifty miles in diameter and the outer sphere is two hundred miles in diameter. The inner sphere will need to withstand a nine G force trying to ingest it. The outer sphere will be at one G. It is simple to make but will need to be assembled in space. Do you have any questions," Zack said as he stopped to let the information sink in?

"This just seems to be getting tougher as I learn more. You said this was the only solution. Don't we have some other weapon at our disposal," the President said looking at Craig?

"There is no weapon known to mankind strong enough to eliminate this black hole from our path. I initially thought Zack had fallen over the edge but when I reviewed his notes and proposed solution, I realized it indeed was the only possible one. This is a problem with only one very difficult monumental solution," Craig responded.

"How much time do I have before I must take action," the President inquired?

"I called you because we are already very late in taking action. We must be on our way toward the black hole in the next two years. You need to understand, accept, and implement this proposal immediately," Craig replied.

"It seems clear to me. It truly is a monumental undertaking. I can see we have the technology to make it happen. I am not sure we have the time and the resources. I agree immediate action is required. I will have my cabinet called together for an emergency meeting on Monday afternoon.

I will send over some resources to help you prepare a presentation. You are planning to work on Sunday while I pray?" the President said as he stood up?

"Yes, we were planning to work tomorrow. Any help we can get would be very useful. Make sure one of them knows all the idiosyncrasies and quirks of your cabinet members. Please apologize for me to Lydia for disturbing her family on the weekend." Craig said as the President got up.

"Craig you always were a pain. I can't say this meeting was a pleasure. This will be a weekend I will probably never forget that I was at Cathy's swim meet when I learned the world was coming to an end," the President said as he opened the office door.

Zack stood looking at the door in disbelief. He had been expecting a long-drawn-out discussion about alternatives. Or at least having the President dig into the details of the discovery.

He looked over at Craig and saw that he was smiling.

"He is that direct and he is very smart. He may be smarter than both of us," Craig said as he commented that they needed to get back to work.

Zack and Craig made an outline of their presentation. They decided to call it a day. They agreed to meet at eight in the morning.

The next morning, Zack was surprised by the number of cars in the parking lot. It was Sunday morning, and the lot was at least half full. He saw Craig's car and parked next to it as usual.

"Good Morning. As you can see, we have lots of help. I have coffee brewing and I have found places for this group from the White House to be able to do their work. I almost left when I drove in and saw all of them here." Craig greeted Zack as he walked in.

"How many are there and what are we going to do with them all," Zack said as he plugged in his laptop?

"There are six of them and they have instructions to prepare the entire presentation. I thought you and I would review what we outlined late yesterday afternoon and then let them go at it. We can do some more work on your design while they get the presentation ready. They can ask questions for clarity and later today we can do the final edit. Tomorrow morning, they can finalize the presentation and make final copy," Craig replied.

"Sounds good to me, I wasn't sure how detailed to make the presentation. They will know exactly what is needed. I am going to introduce myself, get a cup of coffee and then I will be ready to go," Zack replied as his computer came to life.

Monday morning Zack and Craig arrived at the parking lot in the back of the White House. They were stopped at the entrance and asked for identification. Zack was surprised to find their names were on the list. He parked and Craig and he walked up to the entrance gate. Here they were met by one of the team that had worked with them on Sunday on the presentation.

"Welcome to the White House. I'll take you to our office area. We will finalize the presentation and get it ready for the cabinet meeting. We are in the process of finalizing the changes we agreed to yesterday afternoon. Everything is on track. This has personally blown me away. I sure hope your idea takes immediate traction," Jerry the leader of the Presidents team greeted them.

Zack sat down and went through the presentation with Craig. It really was of professional quality.

"Wow, I wonder if this team does any work on the side," Zack commented as they finished the review of the presentation.

The President's team had prepared a simple animated slide presentation showing the black hole, the disappearance of the asteroid, and some education on a black hole. They followed with how the capture and movement of the black hole could happen.

"We should have had this kind of help the last time we were trying to raise money for our studies." Craig commented.

"I agree. We should be able to make a convincing presentation with this slide deck," Zack replied

"I would like you to do the presentation. I will chime in if you miss any critical points, but I would like you to be up front," Craig requested.

Craig was aware that several of the cabinet members did not like the fact that he was a personal friend of the President, and he figured the best course of action was to put Zack out front.

The President walked in and thanked and welcomed everyone for attending this special meeting. He set the stage by asking everyone to allow the entire presentation to be given. Afterwards the group could go back to any point and ask questions.

He pointed to one of the clerks and said that after the presentation ended a paper reference copy would be handed out.

He then introduced Dr. Craig Garrity and Dr. Zackary Milton.

Zack stood and gave a brief introduction of himself.

He then let them know about the discovery of a blackhole that the solar system was approaching.

The presentation went smoothly. The entire room seemed to be at attention and their faces showed no emotion.

The paper copies were handed out as Zack ended the screen presentation.

The President then clarified that he would lead the discussion portion of the meeting.

Zack and Craig listened to the reaction the concept was eliciting from the cabinet members. This was what Zack had anticipated from the President.

"What's the big fuss? Why don't we just send several nuclear missiles and blast the black hole out of the way," the secretary of the interior spoke up loudly.

"Well Lawrence, a black hole can suck in stars and stars that explode with the force of millions of our nuclear missiles. We need to do something very different than to try to apply our meager force. I am also not sure we can be as accurate as we would want from this range," the Secretary of Defense replied.

The response surprised Zack. He sensed the Secretary understood and was supportive of the capture concept.

The discussion which followed allowed Zack to answer additional questions and to share his general approach to capturing and utilizing the black hole.

After, what seemed a redundant and circular discussion the cabinet agreed capturing the black hole was the correct tactical action.

The meeting ended and they followed the President into the oval office.

"The two of you have stepped up to help the world, and I want to thank you. I'm afraid you are in for an experience you did not imagine. Your leadership and guidance are of such critical nature I have asked each of you be assigned personal bodyguards. You will be taken from here directly to FBI headquarters to select them. You may not have noticed but you were being watched since our meeting on Saturday," President Lansing said after the cabinet meeting.

This came as a surprise to both Zack and Craig. They asked whether such action was necessary.

"Please accept this in the spirit of friendship. I have no choice but to ensure your safety. You give me the news of the end of the world and you two are the only ones with the plans to save us. Of course, I have to ensure your safety," the President said as they walked back to his office.

There was no farther discussion on this topic.

"We will need to enroll the leaders of all the major economies. This will be followed by enrolling the entire UN membership. I will arrange for this to happen.

I will have the presentation team, work with you on any tweaks that may be needed. You may need to simplify a few points. I will also need to take part in these next presentations. They will coach all of us on how to best present this concept to ensure getting the global support we need. We are going to have to sell, cajole, beg, sweet talk and threaten. We will need to do whatever it takes to get the key leaders to support us," President Lansing said.

Soon after, Craig and Zack were escorted out to their cars. Two FBI agents got into the back seat and drove home with them.

<u>Chapter 2: Project Savitar</u>

The President stood looking out of his office window. He understood the gravity of the situation and would act with speed and urgency. He had a strong political team, but he had been in office for less than a month and they had barely moved into their offices. He knew that he was taking unprecedented action. He would need all the help from his friends and allies to pull it off.

"Well, I wanted to make a difference. I guess I will need to be careful what I wish for in the future," he thought to himself.

"Mary, come in and let me work with you on some meetings that will need to be immediately scheduled," he said while he held down the speaker button on the intercom to his desk.

Please set up an emergency meeting with the leaders of the Industrial Seven. Set it for Wednesday. Stress, urgency of a global nature needs to be addressed and the requirement for top leader representation.

Tell them I understand this is very unusual, but it is of such a monumental nature that this action is required," Dan clearly instructed.

A week later the leaders sat around the table. By this time the President, Zack and Craig had rehearsed the presentation multiple times.

The President's staff had analyzed each country's most probable objections and the political currency to make alignment happen. One hundred percent agreement was critical. The President knew he needed every leader to be in total support.

"Welcome. Thank You for responding to such a sudden request. I have been as stunned as I believe you will be by what you are going to learn. I have asked Dr. Zachary Milton to explain a serious and very threatening situation. He and his mentor Dr. Craig Garrity have made a startling and grave discovery affecting all of our well-being. I will now let Dr. Milton describe the situation," President Lansing said as he sat down.

"Gentlemen, six months ago, astronomers and scientists verified a small black hole lies ahead of the Earth's path. Our only hope is to capture the black hole and move it out of Earth's way," the Zack said as the picture of a black hole was projected on the screen.

"What is the threat of this black hole on the well-being of the Earth?" President Lansing asked his rehearsed question.

The three had practiced this as means of keeping the discussion moving forward.

"The projected path the of the Earth is so close to the black hole that all surface objects will be stripped off the Earth's surface. The air and the oceans of the planet will be sucked in. The actual planet will pull away and go on its orbital path," Zack replied as the next set of slides animated the words being spoken.

"Is there anything we can do about this situation," President Lansing asked after the buzz had died down?

"Yes, we can move the black hole out of our way," Zack replied as he followed the careful rehearsed script.

"Do you have any idea on how to move a black hole," President Lansing continued?

"Yes, we have a basic design of a cage in which to hold it and then move it out of Earth's path," Zack replied. "In fact, this capture offers a potential platform for long term space exploration."

"Would you please give this group a simple description of how this would be done," the President continued.

Zack turned on a prepared animated video. It showed the black hole, the conceptual capture sphere and simple animation slowly moving the capture sphere around the black hole. Then it went on to show the entire structure being moved out of the path of the Earth.

"The basic idea is to surround the black hole with magnetic fields. We will form a magnetic bottle around the black hole. Then we will slowly push it away from Earth's path.

This will require the construction of a sphere with a fifty-mile inner diameter and an outer shell with a diameter of two-hundred-fifty miles. It will be built it in two halves. These two halves will be closed around the black hole. Giant electromagnets mounted on the sphere will provide the magnetic bottle to hold the black hole," Zack replied.

"My heavens, this will require the total resources of all our countries. Why don't we just blast this thing out of existence," the President responded in mock surprise as he watched several country leaders nod in agreement?

He was now asking the same questions posed during the cabinet briefing. These questions were being asked to allow the leaders around the table to develop a better understanding and some level of initial acceptance.

"Yes, this was our initial reaction until you understand the nature of black holes," Zack responded smoothly. "No matter what we would send in, nothing would ever come back out of a black hole.

Nothing escapes.

Black holes pull in stars. Huge explosions thousands of times more powerful than all our combined weaponry have been documented. The black holes take everything in and actually increase in power and size.

This black hole pulled in a five by ten-mile mile asteroid. The total energy of the asteroids mass is equivalent to all the energy of all our nuclear missiles.

"Our only hope is to capture and hold this small black hole and make it work for us," Zack replied.

"It can be the fire Prometheus gave to man. Harnessed it can make us powerful," Zack orated as he took in the faces around the table.

They were listening. Some were nodding in the affirmative.

"I just hope we are able to move its mass once we capture it," Zack thought as the conversation continued.

None of the scientist on the team was sure as to the mass of the black hole and what power it would take to move it.

The discussion went around the table with questions about the certainty of the observation, of the intercept path, of the amount of time before Earth reached the black hole. It was a repeat of the previous meeting with the cabinet.

"The world has seven years to capture and move this black hole out of Earth's path or we face extinction. We have developed the initial plans of how to build the structure to capture this black hole.

The peoples of Earth have the technology, the capability, and the resources to accomplish this feat. However, it will take all the space going resources our countries can collectively muster," Zack said looking around.

"It will also take the help of all other countries as we essentially built a small city in space," were his final comments.

The muttering and discussion went on for hours. Every objection was discussed and refuted. The mood would swing to agreement and then another objection would be voiced, and the cycle would once again begin.

In the end the President agreed to host the experts from each of these countries for further discussions. He won the concession that the experts would discuss and contribute to initial plans on how to capture the black hole versus debating whether or not to do so.

The meeting came to an end with everyone in agreement. They also decided they would not attend the press conference.

The President sent his press secretary to brief the press and let them know that more would soon be shared. The current line was that a new era of working more closely together had been discussed and some additional time was needed to formalize the message.

"Great job, we will have to thank our staff of coaches. I am exhausted. Let's call it a day and plan on meeting tomorrow morning," President Lansing said to Zack and Craig as the meeting came to an end.

Zack and Craig went home and collapsed. It had truly been an exhausting week.

The next morning, Zack sat across from the President in the oval office. The two were quickly reaching the status of friends. Zack was becoming more at ease in the environment of the White House.

"What should we call this endeavor," asked President Lasing looking over his morning cup of coffee.

He was still feeling the tension of the previous day and the morning coffee was helping to calm his nerves. He was beginning to like this young, brilliant scientist.

"Well, I have thinking of calling it Savitar after the Vedic sun god who urges man and beast to act," Zack replied as he looked back at the President and then glanced at Craig.

He had not discussed the name with Craig. It had come to mind last night on his way home. He hoped Craig was OK with the name. He should have asked before blurting it out.

"What do you think, Craig," Zack quickly asked hoping his mentor and friend would not have a negative reaction.

"Do we really have a chance at capturing this thing and moving it out of our way," the President asked as he intently looked back and forth between the two men?

He sensed Zack's tension and was not sure what the cause might be. He had to have full confidence in these two. They had to be in total agreement. There could be no hidden issues.

"There are no technological barriers in building the needed magnetic bottle. The biggest obstacles will be the monumental logistics of getting everything out into space, assembling our future space exploration platform and having enough time to do it. Time is what we have the least of. To pull it all together will take every rocket, every space launch, thousands of people in space and hundreds of thousands on the ground," Craig replied.

"It will take unprecedented ground resources to gather, assemble and organize all the materials. And all of it must be done in record time. My biggest concern is whether all of this can be kept on track. We need the best project management team Earth can muster," Craig went on.

"The high level of radiation exposure is another formidable obstacle. It will make this journey a death sentence for many of the crew. We need the best radiation shielding possible. However, there will be a great deal of critical external work to be done on the way. I don't know of any way to get around this monumental life-threatening issue and the mortality rate we will experience," Zack spoke up.

He had waited until acceptance to his idea was final before identifying the overwhelming issue on his mind.

"Yes, this issue has been brought up by some of my science advisors. It is the reason we have not yet gone to Mars. They predict a fifty percent or greater fatality rate for a one-way trip out to the black hole. We have no choice. We will need to undertake this journey in spite of this issue," President Lansing said with concern in his voice.

"We need to break this effort into multiple projects. These projects need to converge smoothly a year from now. Each project needs to have a top-level project manager. There needs to be a central super project manager to keep it all on track," Zack continued.

"We need to focus on getting material into orbit, in building the sphere out in space, in building the living quarters and other facilities needed to sustain the crew and the structure. We need to build the equipment to make the magnetic bottle and we need to select and train a crew.

I would like to see Dr. Garrity, and the project management groups coordinate these projects. I will focus on refining the capture scheme, work to see if we can address the radiation issue and in training the crew," Zack spoke quietly.

He had gone through the entire process in his mind and concluded the effort would need a tremendous amount of guidance and discipline if it were to succeed.

"The two of you make it sound like an adventure. I suppose it is the greatest adventure to ever face mankind. My role will be to see the world gets aligned, resources keep coming and the public gets enthused about this venture.

Heaven knows we will spend trillions on this endeavor. I already have my best people developing the PR. Since we will need total commitment, and we cannot afford any misbehavior of either our people or of any country in the world, I will be asking for special powers. Congress must authorize the overall expenditure, but I will use my Presidential power to get this going immediately.

My team is already working to define a way to forge a global alliance. I have already talked privately to the leaders of China, Russia, India, and the EU. We have been aligned in our war on terror. Now it is time to focus on the war of survival. The politics of this will be overwhelming. We are at the center at this historic activity. I am pleased to have a part in all of this," President Lansing replied in an oratory fashion.

It was clear to Zack the President had his heart in the right place and his mind on history and the political opportunity this presented.

"I will have the NASA director, Benjamin Ben Samuelson, come speak to you. He is my choice for overall coordinator of the project. I have communicated this to the other countries, and they agree to work through NASA. NASA will manage the project and set up the training for all personnel going into space and on this journey.

If you intent, on being a member on this mission, you will need astronaut training. Since you are young and in great shape this will get you ready to lead this expedition. That is what you seek isn't it, Zack," President Lansing asked?

Zack was stunned and was unable to give an immediate reply. He had not thought about leading the effort.

"What about you Craig? Are you planning to go as well," the President continued?

He knew Emily, Craig's wife, and the close relationship the two shared and wondered whether Craig would want to go.

"I will take the training, but we are going to need an anchor here on Earth to ensure everything science can learn in the next few years about managing and handling a black hole gets learned.

I see Zack as the right person to be in charge of the expedition. Savitar is a great name for this project and the space vessel," Dr. Garrity replied with a twinkle in his eye.

Craig appreciated Zack's sensitivity about picking a name without discussing it with him first. He was not surprised at Zack's inability to answer the President about leading the effort. The subject had not come up until this moment. He was pleased Dan saw in Zack what Craig already knew was there.

"I imagine every country will fight for a spot on the crew. You will need to determine every crew member's role and how many you will need. I don't think you will have a shortage of volunteers. You will probably need to limit the number and select the members to ensure the countries participating all get represented. NASA will also serve as the recruiting center. You should concentrate on the volunteers and on determining if the persons offered fit. NASA will provide you with all the psychologists, screeners, and clearances," President Lansing continued.

"Things will take off very fast. I am sure there will be times you think you have totally lost control. Let's plan to meet every other week. In this way you will be able to share your firsthand observations and provide me some critical insider calibration. I will provide you with influence in the coming circus of events.

Ben Samuelson will contact you in the next day or two," President Lansing said as he stood, indicating it was time for them to leave

"Events are really skyrocketing along. Did I just get put in charge to lead this effort?" Zack asked as he and Craig were escorted out of the White House.

"Yes, Zack the President did make the selection. He recognizes the project will continue well after the Savitar leaves the Earth," Craig replied with a chuckle.

Zack was thrilled by the fact both Craig and the President agreed he would lead the project. Random thought fragments about the project flashed through his mind. He felt intoxicated.

Two men dressed in dark blue business suits met them at the exit. The two showed them their shields and identified themselves as FBI agents.

"We are members of the presidential staff. We are to take you to FBI headquarters. You will meet with the head of the FBI and then you are to begin interviewing to select your personal bodyguards." Bill the older of the two explained.

"Well, the President warned us about this. Is it really necessary?" Zack asked.

"Evidently it is. Whatever you are into has already made the internet. You guys have already gotten some threats, and no one even knows what you are doing. All we know is it is about national security. Sorry guys if you haven't had security coverage before you may find us to be pests. I hope you are up to this since it will last for as long as we can foresee," the older of the two continued as they walked out to a black limousine.

The trip to the FBI headquarters took them through the nation's mall. Here all the symbols of power and American history seemed to reflect the importance of the moment. Zack and Craig sat quietly as they were driven toward the FBI offices.

"The bureau has done the initial selection of the candidates. The best of the best, all the brainy types or the best bodyguards with a chance of understanding what the two of you are doing were selected. All have undergone psychological checks and have had their security backgrounds rechecked. They will be with you twenty-our seven. I would guess they are all young, bright, single, and truly the best. Every one of them is probably dying to get picked. Take your time and make sure you get along with them before finalizing your selection. Sleep on it overnight." the oldest of the agents a

Thank you for reading this far.

Continue by reading **Savitar**.

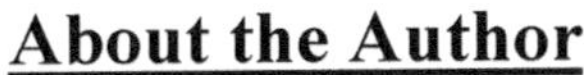

About the Author

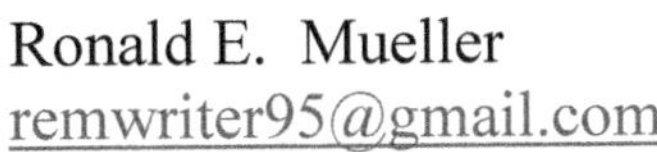

Ronald E. Mueller
remwriter95@gmail.com

Ron grew up in what is now Flint River State Park in Southeast Iowa. The 170-year-old house Ron lived in is built into a hillside. It faces a 125-foot-high cliff towering over the little Flint River. The house and the land talked to him about; the passing of time, the struggle to conquer the land, the struggles people faced and the wonder of nature.

He climbed the cliffs, crawled into the caves, dove from the swimming rock, collected clams from the bottom of the pond, gigged and skinned frogs for their legs. He trapped muskrats for fur, hunted raccoon in the dead of night, and with only a stick hunted rabbits in the dead of winter.

His young life was outdoors, and nature tested him.

He walked to a one room stone schoolhouse uphill both ways. A stern but warm-hearted teacher Mrs. Henry was instrumental in shaping his character as she shepherded him from the fourth to the eighth grade. A Montessori before its time. It was a fantastic way to grow up.

His experiences inter-twined with snippets of fantasy lend themselves to the adventures he leads the reader through.

322

Journey's End

Ron Mueller

Published by: Around the World Publishing LLC.

QR Links to
ATWP.US web site